F. SCOTT FITZGERALD:
AMERICAN SPY

Other books by Murray Sinclair

Tough Luck L.A.

Only in L.A.

Goodbye L.A.

F. SCOTT FITZGERALD: AMERICAN SPY

A NOVEL

MURRAY SINCLAIR

Eclectic
BOOKS

Eclectic Books, Los Angeles, California
For information, email Eclectic Books at murray@murraysinclairlaw.com
or go to facebook.com/MurrayMSinclair

Book cover and interior design by
Jessica Shatan Heslin/Studio Shatan, Inc.

Book cover and interior illustrations by Rick Geary

Library of Congress Cataloging-in-Publication Data is to come.

ISBN 979-8-986-82610-3 (hardcover)
ISBN 979-8-986-82611-0 (paperbook)
ISBN 979-8-986-82612-7 (ebook)

For my grandson Sydney F. Sinclair

"Trust thyself: every heart vibrates to that iron string."

—Ralph Waldo Emerson, "Self Reliance"

F. SCOTT FITZGERALD: AMERICAN SPY

FOREWORD

Whether the following pages be fact or fiction, there can be no doubt that they will intrigue any inquisitive, well-informed reader. That they exist at all is a minor miracle.

Five years ago, on a Sunday afternoon in the Spring of 1978, Harvey Ratchman, a retired electrical engineer, attended the Washington, DC garage sale of Mrs. Beth McDonald, a kindly widow in her late seventies, whose grown children had come from out of town to assist her in cleaning out her apartment house before its sale became complete by the close of the escrow period. Mrs. McDonald was planning to move in with her daughter, after having resided on the premises as owner-manager for over forty-five years. While browsing among the garage sale items, Mr. Ratchman came across a very heavy trunk of papers. It was in good condition and—as it wasn't tagged—he inquired about the price. Negotiations ensued between Mr. Ratchman and Mrs. McDonald's daughter, and a nominal amount was agreed upon.

As Mr. Ratchman emptied the trunk's contents in a large trash box, Mrs. McDonald approached and spoke at great length to Mr. Ratchman of the trunk's previous owner. His name was Hyman Skolski. Mr. Skolski, according to Mrs. McDonald, had been a member of the French Resistance. He resided with Mrs. McDonald in a rear upstairs bachelor apartment from June 15, 1940 until February, 1942. He had asked Mrs. McDonald to keep his locked trunk in storage until he sent for it. He never did.

At this point, Mr. Ratchman perused the papers he was emptying into the trash. He thought they were handwritten in a foreign language—perhaps Polish, because of Mr. Skolski's surname. Mrs. McDonald knew nothing about the papers, as she had never seen them. Her son had just opened the trunk that morning, snipping off the key lock with a pair of wire cutters. Mr. Ratchman was curious. It occurred to him that the papers might contain information of historic interest.

Determined to find out, Mr. Ratchman placed Mr. Skolski's papers back into the trunk. He took the trunk home. During the next week, Mr. Ratchman was painstakingly thorough in his research, but he could not find any language which approx-

imated the language of Mr. Skolski's papers. That was when he realized the writing was in code.

Working systematically, Mr. Ratchman approached the code as if he were looking for crossed or faulty wiring in a piece of tricky electrical circuitry. Five months later, he had broken the code, thus rendering it into French, a foreign language he neither spoke nor understood. He acquired the services of Daphne Ellis, a retired foreign language instructor, and the two of them labored diligently over the next six months, translating the documents from French into English. Working from Mr. Ratchman's code, the documents have been re-translated by Raymond Kaufman of Columbia University, for this edition, resulting in a somewhat more elegant refinement of expression.

We owe much to Mr. Ratchman's dedication and tenacity—without his efforts, this volume of elusive operative Henri Duval's fascinating historical correspondence to Hyman Skolski would not be available to readers. The information contained herein undoubtedly sheds new light on both literary and world history. Many will say the documents are a hoax. But having been consulted in the preparation of this book in an editorial fact-checking capacity, I could not, in good conscience, recommend its publication if I thought it a fraud. For even though we have had difficulty in confirming Henri Duval's activities in L'Esprit Libre, his Resistance group, Duval's role as one of the founders of the organization has been authenticated. And we are fairly certain that he lived in Hollywood during the period of this correspondence (his name is listed in the employment records of Paramount Studios[1]). Although F. Scott Fitzgerald

1. Accounts Payable, Paramount Studios, August-October, 1940; courtesy of Paramount Studios Archives.

makes no express reference in any of his writings to any clandestine liaison with Duval, the French Resistance, or any political faction, his political sentiments are strongly expressed in
his communications with family and friends in the last year of
his life.

Still, we cannot confirm the surreptitious activities alleged
in Duval's letters. In addition, from further inquiry, we know
of no extant person of Fitzgerald's acquaintance who ever met
Duval or saw Duval and Fitzgerald together. However, we have
scrutinized the dates, times, people, and events portrayed in
these documents, and, though we do not possess unequivocal
proof of their veracity, we cannot refute their hypothetical existence in fact by citing incontrovertible evidence of things it has
been documented that Mr. Fitzgerald did in their place.

In short, the ultimate judgment belongs to the discerning
reader and future historians.

BERTRAND B. SLOAN
Princeton University
November 1983

Hollywood, California
June 25, 1940

Dear Hyman,

It feels like a lifetime since I've had a decent meal with drink-able wine. Here, they look at you like you're crazy if you order anything aside from a sickening-sweet milkshake, watery beer, or terrible whisky. I've given up trying to get wine, even in the better restaurants. It's too much of a chore. Even the French varieties have already turned.

Americans. If we didn't need them so desperately, you couldn't pay me to set foot here. I agree with you that they are an uncivilized, barbarous race. As you've said, there is no sense of balance in them (with my architectural training, I can also see this in their buildings—more on that later). They do not know how to savor pleasure or sustain enjoyment. They are for-ever guilt-ridden and Puritanical. My close study of the Ameri-can writer-type personified by F. Scott Fitzgerald indicates that, when it comes to drinking, they are either entirely against it, or they indulge to such destructive excess that it kills them even as they live. They are worse than the French—if you can believe it.

Enough philosophizing. My finances are holding up well. I've been living in the lap of luxury, as the Americans say. My residence is a celebrity hotel that goes by the exotic name of the Garden of Allah. It is quite beautiful in a very second-class sort of way—a collection of large, Spanish-style stucco bungalows clustered about a large pool that is supposedly shaped like the Black Sea because its original owner, a Russian silent-screen actress named Alla Nazimova, wanted something to remind her of home.

The Garden of Allah is typical of this place called Hollywood. Everywhere, the buildings are stage sets—from log cabins to chateaus. The average people are "fans" (short for fanatic, in case you didn't know), meaning they're madly happiest when they're trying to live out their fantasies of their favorite stars. Their fashion and hairstyles follow the latest movies. Crazy, isn't it?

As to the stars themselves, many stay at this hotel when they're visiting from New York on assignments with the film studios. Or they live here permanently if they don't want the responsibility of keeping up a home or apartment. The Garden of Allah is a good place for them to be seen, too. That's what these people are always doing—keeping up their images, and making show business contacts to advance their careers. They have to. The Garden of Allah is expensive—my room is $100 per week. Many of them have been involved in scores of pictures, but they must spend every cent they make. Which is why they move in and out daily. It costs a great deal to live as if you are always putting on a show.

But this is the perfect place for me. In addition to the occasional stars, many other successful show businesspeople—particularly writers—live here. I am just a block away from Mr. Fitzgerald's apartment.

Who would guess that the rest of the world is in the middle

"MY RESIDENCE IS A CELEBRITY HOTEL THAT GOES BY THE NAME OF THE GARDEN OF ALLAH."

of a war? It's all over the papers, but here, you don't hear people talking about it around the pool or on the street. Of course, we go everywhere by car, mostly, so there isn't much time for conversation or sustained thought. And there aren't any real *cafes*, where you can run into friends and sit and talk without a waitress hovering over you, check in hand, as other people stare, tapping their toes and waiting for your seat.

What a godforsaken place. But at least it's generally cheerful (the weather is wonderful!) and the Americans are strong. They would never lack for courage—nor would they ever let themselves lapse into a state of unpreparedness. Because they do not seem to have learned how to relax or enjoy their existence, they are vigilant, watchful, and resourceful in preparing for some nearly accessible, just-out-of-reach future in which happiness, love, prosperity, and passion will freely reign in startling, endless abundance. They are a self-sufficient people—that much I can say for them. They may have wrapped themselves in a waking dream-cloud—as evidenced by their hysteria for the cinema—but dreaming too much is better than not dreaming at all. Wouldn't you agree? When was the last time our average Frenchman dreamed that he was anything but an ass-wipe for a German rear?

Of course, I have seen all the papers. The headlines say the war has ended for us and that we are in mourning for our "dead lost cause." Don't you love it? Doesn't it make you laugh that the great Marshal Philippe Pétain says that we are "certain to show greater grandeur in avowing our defeat than in opposing vain and illusory projects"? Gandhi, I must quote: "What is going on before our eyes is a demonstration of the futility of violence and also of Hitlerism. I think French statesmen have shown real courage in bowing to the inevitable and refusing to be party to mutual slaughter."

Piss on them both! France is not dead if the two of us—at least—are in health and sound of mind.

Your friend,
Henri

Hollywood
June 26, 1940

Dear Hyman,

I'm so damned bored and anxious here, waiting for the proper moment to contrive my introduction to Mr. Fitzgerald. I hardly know what to do with myself when I'm not writing you letters. I hope you don't mind. Our correspondence helps me to clarify my thinking. I feel confident our security is good. I will use the code always. If there are any problems that I should know about, you know the other way to reach me.

I will be the first to admit the irony of our respective positions. You are the writer, yet I have ended up in Hollywood doing my best to impersonate one. Perhaps it's better this way. Most of the other writers here are impostors, too, except they don't know it. They tell me that they sit around in teams of two or three on couches, telling each other stories and trying to make up catchy dialogue that they throw back and forth to their shared secretary. She records it on a machine, types up what sounds best to her, and then everybody goes home.

Is this writing? Is this the search for Flaubert's *le mot juste?* Some of them work together in their hotel rooms. There are two guys next door to me. Yesterday, after I wrote to you, I lis-

tened to them through the wall. They yelled so much and used
so much slang, I couldn't make sense of the story they were
working on. It had something to do with what they call a "Western," with cowboys and Indians and such. I heard a young lady
screaming as a man shouted that he wanted to lasso a cow. I've
since discovered that a lasso is a rope cowboys use to catch
cattle or horses.

Then gunshots went off.

I did what any ordinary man would do in such a situation.
I ran next door. But I discovered a party. There were almost
twenty people there! Three men wore Western clothes, Stetson hats, bandanas around their necks, boots with spurs, and
leather leggings over their trousers. Two of them were twirling
old-fashioned six-shooters, firing them with blank charges and
laughing. One of these cowboys had a thick greasepaint moustache, and he'd used the same stuff to darken his eyebrows. The
one without the six-shooters wore a curly blond wig. He was the
one with the lasso, encircling a young lady with platinum blond
hair. It was extremely loud and hectic, but the theme of this
gathering seemed to have to do with these silly-looking men
and their costumes. They solicited the small crowd's opinion of
their appearance and were anxious whether they looked funny.

They call themselves the Marx Brothers, I found out—
Groucho, Harpo, and Chico—and they are very popular in
American comedy cinema. I can't make sense of them, but
they're very nice fellows. They enjoyed themselves immensely
making fun of my heavy French accent. Groucho enjoyed it
the most. He thought it very heroic of me to rush in to save the
maiden in distress, and he introduced me to the platinum-haired
girl who had been screaming and told her to find out what is so
great about French lovers. He kept rushing around the room,

wagging his cigar. Then he'd come back to the girl and myself and ask us nonsense questions about my amorous aptitude.

"Have you always been a great lover?" he said. Before I could answer, he interjected, "I've always loved her, too, but it led to divorce." He turned back to the girl. "I loved her, and he loved her. They all loved her. But why did she love him?"

It didn't make much sense, but it was very funny at the time, though it flustered the girl. It's the only time I can remember enjoying being the butt of someone else's joke. I'm starting to feel a special kinship with these Americans—for soon, if all goes according to plan, they will give their flesh and blood to our cause. And there's something else, I suppose. Have I said these people have the innocence of puppies? They're so fresh and sprightly—even the adults are like children or idiots. They smile when they walk down the street. It's a little frightening.

But back to Mr. Groucho Marx. I left the impromptu affair a few hours later, and had just gotten into bed when someone knocked on my door. It was the young lady from the party. She giggled and said Groucho had sent her for research into foreign affairs. She liked to giggle. I didn't go to bed with her, though she was most ravishing. There have already been numerous opportunities for such dalliances, but I am trying to cultivate an image, am I not?

The writers, as I have observed, are a merry but puritanical lot. Most of them seem to be married. Few would entertain the notion of having more than one mistress at a time. Especially Mr. Fitzgerald. It is important that I begin my association with the man from a position of respect, so that the two of us have things in common. Therefore, I am wearing a wedding band. I have also bought the same model car as his—a 1934 Ford coupe—for $140. Americans enjoy talking about their cars. Mr.

Fitzgerald is sure to find it a fascinating coincidence, and one that should prove a fruitful topic of conversation.

After sending Mr. Marx's lady friend away, I was asleep finally by around 1 a.m., when I was awakened by another knock. It was another woman this time—a tall brunette. "Groucho sent me," she said. I told her I was in bed, and she offered to join me. When I asked her why, she looked surprised and said that she thought I was another writer on the new picture. I told her I didn't know a thing about the new picture, and she left.

Six other women knocked at my door over the next few hours. They were of every description—from twenty to eighty years of age. I was no longer amused. When I opened my door for what I'd decided was the last time, it was Mr. Groucho Marx. Except for his greasepaint, bandana, Stetson hat, and boots with spurs, he was nude! He had a six-shooter in each hand. He asked me if I was married. I lied, answering in the affirmative. He shot off both guns, said, "That explains it," and walked away.

Ten minutes later, someone knocked again. It was a policeman in a blue uniform.

"You're under arrested," he told me.

I grinned at his seeming malapropism. "For what?" I asked.

"Development," he said, breaking character with a chuckle. "Groucho says no Frenchman in his right mind could ever be so much in love . . . with his wife, that is."

He said Groucho was sorry for having disturbed me, and then laughed and walked away.

I should have plucked one of those succulent plums, perhaps. I don't want these people to stop thinking I'm French.

Your friend,
Henri

Dear Hyman,

Breakfast in bed this morning, along with a pair of earmuffs, a sleep mask, satin pajamas, and a matching smoking jacket—all courtesy of Mr. Groucho Marx. "Sleep tight—perchance to dream," said the accompanying note. I gave the bellboy a generous tip.

When I knocked on Mr. Marx's door later to thank him, I almost didn't recognize him. He wore a suit of dark pinstripes. He and another man were going over some of the plot difficulties in their new story. The mood was one of sober deliberation. I was invited to join them.

The other man was the writer of the new film. I cannot remember his name, but he seemed upset with Mr. Marx. Both smoked heavy cigars. We sat in a cloud of smoke as the writer told Mr. Marx that it was too late to change the story again, since they were scheduled to begin the production the next day. Mr. Marx said he didn't care. He was worried that the story wasn't funny enough. He gave me a copy of the script and asked me to read it. I said I would be glad to take it with me, but Mr. Marx demanded that I read it to them now. I opened the script and started with the description of the first scene. It was in a dancehall. Mr. Marx slapped his knee and roared with laughter.

He said it was the funniest thing he'd ever heard and that they would do the whole story with French accents now. The writer told Mr. Marx he was crazy. Mr. Marx dropped onto the floor and bit the writer's leg.

When he settled down a while later, he wanted us to think of funny things that could happen in gold prospecting. Trying to mimic Mr. Marx's odd sense of humor, I suggested that the miners could find radioactive fool's gold that could turn them into slavering idiots. Mr. Marx thought this was the most brilliant thing he'd ever heard, but the other man wasn't sure it would function within the context of their story. Mr. Marx concocted scenarios for anyone who had been exposed to the fool's gold. He was a charming, childish man. I enjoyed watching his antics.

After some time, Mr. Marx's brothers arrived, and they taught me to play poker. We played for matchsticks only, but still there was much arguing, and now—though it has been hours since I left them—my ears are still ringing from their loud voices.

I am sorry I have not gotten much accomplished, but at least I'm establishing myself as a scenarist. I have been reading various books on the craft of writing for the cinema so I will not embarrass myself once I begin work at one of the Hollywood studios (a job the Minister of Foreign Affairs is in the process of arranging for me).

As far as the organization of Pétain's new government, it does not cease to amaze me how well set up everything is already. You can't help but think that the apologists prepared or even planned France's fall long ago. We shall have our revenge.

Your friend,
Henri

Dear Hyman,

I am a touch jittery. In around an hour, I am going to a dinner dance at which I shall attempt to make my first acquaintance with Mr. Fitzgerald. A few of the writers here at the Garden have been discussing the event for days. I heard one of them (Robert Benchley, a well-known American humorist) mention that Scott Fitzgerald would be sitting at his table.

The dinner dance is a fundraiser for the American Peace Mobilization. This organization used to call itself the American Anti-Nazi League. I'm not sure, but this change in designation may have something to do with the Hitler-Stalin pact, for most of those opposed to Germany are also card-carrying communists. Now that Hitler and Stalin are buddies, they will be against America entering the war.

The writers around the hotel have mentioned the importance of attending these affairs. One fellow who works at Metro-Goldwyn-Mayer told me he got that job by attending a charity dinner to raise money to buy ambulances for the Spanish Loyalists in their last war. He didn't know anything about the cause, but many of Hollywood's most powerful producers attend such affairs, so he decided to go and "hobnob" with them. A Metro producer had indigestion and asked this fellow to dance with his wife. Well, one thing led to another (not with the wife—she wasn't very attractive) and the Metro producer was so taken with this writer and appreciative of his etiquette that he asked him to come to the studio the following Monday.

This anecdote was for my benefit, I assume, since I'd let it be known that I was seeking employment. I retell it for our mutual edification, and to illustrate what I feel about this peculiar lotus land. There is a certain inauthenticity about show-business people. They do not seem to stand or care for anything—they only want to impress each other with their sharp wits or new-found wealth. I suppose they are not unlike most of us, but I find them so exceedingly self-obsessed that it is a rather hard thing to become accustomed to.

Saw a film last night—*Confessions of a Nazi Spy*—with the famous gangster star Edward G. Robinson playing an FBI agent (or "G-Man") who exposes a Nazi spy network in the United States. The production was nearly shut down while it was being filmed, due to various attempts to sabotage the sets and threaten (anonymously, of course) the actors. I have been told that the German consulate's Nazi *charge d'affaires* here (Hans Thomsen) denounced the film as "pernicious propaganda" before it was released. Yet this morning I told a handful of my new acquaintances I had seen the movie, without voicing an opinion other than that I found it "interesting"—and all of them voiced unequivocal disdain, calling it simple-minded, melodramatic, and (except for the well-respected Robinson) overacted. The Nazis, they felt, were crudely drawn—in real life they are not as blatantly evil as Harry Warner (the head of Warner Brothers Studios and the valiant soul responsible for this film) had made them out to be. I looked up some reviews, including one from that august publication, the *New York Times*, which said essentially the same thing.

Of course, these people are in for a very big surprise. If any-thing, this entertainment was an understatement. The Nazis *are* obvious, and there is no level to which their ignominious reign of terror will not descend. They will say or do anything. Yet our leaders are not listening. It is plain to see how urbanity, sophistication, subtle intelligence, and perhaps even genius can hinder the most rudimentary common sense.

The comics show a firmer grasp of the matter. I read them to improve my colloquial usage and slang. In one, called *Joe Palooka*, our hero is a punch-drunk ex-boxer. Two Sundays ago, he was walking down the street when he saw a bunch of bullies picking on a little kid. Joe asks why they're being so mean to this little boy, who only yesterday was their friend. He's told that a man named "Big" gave them a list of names of kids who are "yella and ain't like us and don't belong." Joe confronts Big and tells him he's teaching "hatred and intolerance and un-Ameri-canism." When Big attacks him from behind, he kicks Big's ass around the block. The message is that "Kids don't know hatred. Grown-ups has t' teach 'em."

Then in last Sunday's strip, Joe gives the kids a history lesson, in which he credits the French (Lafayette) for helping America fight for democracy. There's a caricature of Hitler, with HATE SOCIETY on his armband, and Uncle Sam tells Bigotry and Intol-erance to "Get out of here!" Joe goes on to tell the kids, "This become the Grandiest place on earth because the people here was brothers. An' when anybody preaches hatred of another person—becuz his hair is darker or becuz he don't folla the next fella's type of belief—then he's anti-american an' tryin' t' destroy our country. So let's keep hatred outa this country, fellas. Don't forget—Hatred fer one kind winds up hatred fer all kinds!"

Americans do talk like this, in part, but I haven't heard anybody around here make as much sense as Joe Palooka. It will be interesting to attend the dinner and find out more about the prevailing Hollywood attitude. As I have said, I think I understand them. Those who are thoughtful and refined cannot conceive of such rancorous, benighted barbarism. But there are those for whom the politics are merely a starting point, a means to an end, as they must have some "serious" excuse to justify getting together and socializing. It eases their consciences if they think they are doing it all for some just cause.

But I'm jumping far ahead of myself, aren't I? I have not even been to this dinner yet and already I'm telling you all about it.

We shall see. I would like to go for a short swim now, but the pool is closed. I don't know why I'm telling you this, except that there are thousands of little goldfish swimming about in the pool. There is a purifying chemical in the water and it is killing them. The person who put the goldfish in thought it would be funny, I suppose. But it is absurd, like these people and this environment. The little fish seem heedless. You cannot tell if they know they are dying. This water is strange, but there is no other place for them to go. They are like the French, the Jews, the Poles—all our dear refugees of the fallen continent. And those who have put them there laugh. To them it is a joke, a diversion. They are abysmally horrible creatures—wretched in mind, body, and spirit—who cannot live with themselves. And when these fish die, their tormentors will, like a cat who has grown bored sporting with a mouse, find something else to distract them from their cares.

Neither was *Confessions of a Nazi Spy* an exaggeration of the Nazi problem regarding the infiltration of German agents. Shouldn't I know? For tangentially, at least, am I not one of them in my capacity as Assistant Foreign Minister for France's new provisional government? I would be worried if my activities and contacts were linked to the German underground in the US. But Pétain (or Laval and the others), thankfully, is not going that far, at least not yet—and it is doubtful that the Germans will ever allow us into their inner circle. It is tragic, pitiful, and appalling that we cannot see this from the start. Germany will never be our friend. What they expect me to do—to contact the US's Axis-sympathetic press and tell them charming stories about the boundless kindness of the German conquerors; to tell them we expect that Europe will soon find peace; to blame the war on Great Britain—how it makes me ill! I have performed my official duty on a few occasions already, with the subtle strategic hope of getting access to the Nazi spy community, so I know whom to watch out for. But the door is locked to me, and no one offers assistance. I will have to make my way groping in the dark. But I do feel they are here, and I intend to be extremely cautious. Pétain or Laval may even have people lurking behind me, looking over my shoulder. It's doubtful, but who knows?

Your friend,
Henri

Dear Hyman,

I went to that dinner dance in Hollywood a few nights ago given by the organization that calls itself the American Peace Mobilization. As you know, I am not a political thinker (thank God) and have no aspiration of becoming one. But I do pride myself in possessing a modicum of common sense—a quality of mind obviously lacking in these great American Hollywood "artists."

I met Mr. F. Scott Fitzgerald, who is presently driving us north toward the California border, after we spent the night in a dingy Tijuana motel—but more about that momentarily. (Please excuse my writing—this Ford has a *very* bumpy ride, much worse than mine.) As I think I said in the last letter, the American Peace Mobilization was formed to replace the American Anti-Nazi League after the infamous Nazi-Soviet pact was made known and it was no longer deemed chic to be opposed to Germany—according to the American Communist Party. You see, most members of this group are communists. They were the majority in the old Anti-Nazi League and they're unanimous in this Peace Mobilization organization.

It's very sad, actually, because so many of them are basically nice people, but unfortunately, they possess the overdeveloped minds of intellectuals. They know much, which ultimately results in so very little. Like the musclebound weightlifters I have seen while running on the beach in Santa Monica, they seem smart, but are so tied up in the interstices of their confused thoughts that they haven't the mental strength to swat a fly. The greatest tragedy for an intelligent man is when he becomes more interested in ideas than people. These pitiful political dilettantes (many of whom are refugees themselves!) accept the party line that Poland was invaded for the sake of the Polish people and that France was not—and England is not—fighting fascism in opposing the Nazis. To them, the war is simply an imperialist struggle between money-grubbing capitalist countries, and Russia is buying time by *pretending* to be Germany's friend. Ha! These communists might as well be Nazis for all the sense they make. I am so disgusted; I cannot tell you. My head is so hot as I write you, it feels as if steam must be coming out of my ears!

Someone named Dorothy Parker handed me a pamphlet entitled, "Let's Skip the Next War." Its headline was "NO WAR for the USA, But a House and Lot for Everyone." These attitudes were expressed in the speech given by the keynote speaker for the evening, a writer named Jack Lawson. Perhaps he is anti-Semitic, but I don't think so. He thinks mankind will be best served by keeping America out of the war. Again, that's the party line. Not everyone thinks this way, of course, but most do. I wouldn't give these pitifully ignorant cranks a second thought if it were not for the fact that they seem representative of the Hollywood writer's current state of mind—and Mr. Fitzgerald himself seems dangerously under their sway, I'm afraid. He associates with and seems greatly impressed by them. Due to the current precariousness of his reputation in the literary community, he seems willing to say or do anything so that people will like him and assume that he can dash off these fatuous scenarios in his sleep whilst never compromising his true literary tastes and aspirations. I hope to exploit this somewhat desperate impulse to our advantage.

All is not lost, though, as far as the man's political sympathies. He wants his literary friends—like Dorothy Parker and her husband, Alan Campbell, Donald Stewart, and others—to think he's a communist. But in the time I've already spent with him I've noticed that he is possessive about France and Great Britain, and contemptuous of the Germans, whom he likens to offensive, churlish, prurient bullies. He has a boyish fascination with history, seeing the great battles as spectacular chess games in which brilliant tacticians manipulate little tin men. War isn't real to him. He hasn't been close enough to understand it. Of course, neither have I—but I know the empty humiliation of losing one's country and losing the freedom and dignity we thought was as natural and inalienable as breathing fresh air.

Mr. Fitzgerald is the same way about his politics as he is about his history. Like any man of deep feeling and sensitivity, he possesses a sincere desire for a better world. He is interested in utopian thinkers—but he is ambivalent, too, fortunately. Regardless of the party line, he *is* rooting for the Allies to win the war, if America doesn't have to be a part of it. This way, the aspiring American communist can have his cake and eat it too. Europe can be saved but America will not be called upon to intervene directly. As I say, the man is confused. At heart, he is not communist, and he despises the Nazis. He should be intelligent enough to know that America's entry is nothing more than a matter of time. But like most Americans, he doesn't understand the fundamentals of the situation. What is so utterly unpardonable is this sloughing off of responsibility. This idea that one may root for England and throw them a bone in aid, but it is *their* war, *their* obligation. They must pick themselves up by their bootstraps. In the meantime, too many lives will be lost, and France is living in disgrace!

I have not argued yet with Mr. Fitzgerald. I am letting him do most of the talking. It has worked so far. He thinks I am interested only in saving my own skin, and it bothers him, which is good. Mr. Fitzgerald is a man who demands large gestures from life. Frenchmen are patriots, and he won't have it any other way. He's gotten himself stirred up, I think, trying to convince me to fight back. He'd be the last to admit it, but part of him wants to join in the fighting already.

Now, let me tell you how I ended up here in Mr. Fitzgerald's car in Tijuana.

After the red-tinged dinner speech at the Hollywood gathering, a large orchestra came out and they opened the dance floor. Mr. Fitzgerald and his date were up and foxtrotting as soon as the music started. Mr. Fitzgerald wore a dark blue suit with a striped tie and oxford cloth shirt. The suit was a little shiny on the pants seat and elbows—and so was Mr. Fitzgerald on the top. His pale blond hair, like my dark brown, is thinning on the crown. His date was a nice-looking doll with a full shape—just the way I like them. She wore a black satin gown, buttoned along the side, all the way to the cut-off collar—Oriental style. She had a white and yellow orchid in her dark blond hair.

I overheard someone talking about her, and I had my background information on her already. Her name is Sheilah Graham. She is younger and prettier than the other Hollywood gossip columnists. A hot little number. It wouldn't be hard to go for her, but she looked like a snob, and she didn't move very well either, at least not the way Mr. Fitzgerald seemed to want. They danced stiffly. He pulled at her, she pulled at him, and she'd finally come his way. They were awkward, uncertain, looking all around and making chit-chat with the other couples on the floor until they got going; then they danced cheek to cheek, and he patted her rear once or twice for good measure. He whispered in her ear at length. She pulled away from him then. He looked alarmed, then composed himself and caught up with her as she marched away—hoping no one noticed her burst from the sanctuary of his foxtrotting embrace. He followed her back to their table. After she shunned him by quickly entering a conversation with others of their group, he sulked off toward the lobby.

I caught up with him in the restroom. I didn't see him at first. Then I saw that one of the stalls was shut, and his pant legs and the tips of his shoes were visible underneath, sticking out beyond the closed door, where they shouldn't have been if he had been sitting or standing at the toilet. I heard a soft *glug-glug*. He was drinking! Probably from either a hip flask or a half-pint bottle.

I took my time at the urinal, then moved over to the sink and washed my hands. I wasn't sure what to do next. I thought maybe I should go into one of the stalls and stay there until Mr. Fitzgerald came out. While using the modern hand dryer, with its forced hot air, I tried to nerve myself into starting all over in one of the stalls, when suddenly Mr. Fitzgerald's door swung back and he stepped out, rubbing the sleeve of his blue blazer across his mouth, and then drawing his lips in so that, for a brief moment, he looked toothless, before smacking them loudly like a cowboy spitting tobacco into a spittoon.

When he saw me, he coughed to cover his embarrassment.

Then, without so much as a nod, he walked to the long mirror above the sinks and scrutinized himself. He fell into a little trance—expecting, I suppose, that I had already taken my leave of him. Now *I* coughed, and approached the row of sinks, where I combed my own thinning hair, and labored diligently to get Mr. Fitzgerald to meet my gaze in the mirror. When he did so, I pretended I had just noticed him. I nodded politely and lifted my brows in courteous salute, as embarrassed genteel strangers are wont to do when meeting by happenstance. Mr. Fitzgerald's brow furrowed. His lips pursed together again, this time into a judgmental look. He seemed to dislike me on sight. Or was it just my imagination?

I went back to combing my hair. Then I made as if I had just realized something. I dropped my jaw, held my comb suspended in mid-air, and turned toward Mr. Fitzgerald.

"Excuse me," I said. "You aren't Mr. F. Scott Fitzgerald, are you?"

"No, I am not," answered F. Scott Fitzgerald. "Who is he?"

"Only the greatest living American writer."

He had been looking at me askance in the mirror. Now, he turned to meet my gaze. His brow was no longer thoughtfully furrowed, but formed a definite scowl. The corners of his mouth were downturned with dissatisfaction, and you could see little tremors of tension in the stony, set, bulldog-like impassivity of his lips. He was very angry—for what reason, I did not yet know.

"What's that accent?" he demanded.

"I am French," I said politely, trying to sound apologetic—I was beginning to suspect it was my accent that appalled him so forcefully. I smiled broadly and went on, determined to win him over. "Mr. Fitzgerald, I can't tell you how much I—"

"Have you summered at Cap d'Antibes?"

"Yes, many times. Why do you ask?"

"When?"

"Oh, through the years. Forgive me. Let me introduce my—"

"What about the summer of 1924?"

"That's so long ago." I smiled. I felt miffed, but was determined to be pleasant.

"Not for me."

I paused, trying to recollect. Perhaps we had a common bond?

"Well?" he demanded.

"Yes," I said, though I wasn't sure. "I think so—definitely. Have we—"

Even though I suspected Mr. Fitzgerald was displeased with my accent, my presence (perhaps I had interrupted his train of thought or his stealthy drinking), or my general appearance, I didn't expect him to pummel me. But he did.

It came out of nowhere. A nearly full bottle of gin fell out of the inside pocket of his jacket, crashed raucously on the tile floor, and shattered as he telegraphed an extremely weak, wide overhand right-left combination to my jaw. It felt like I had a lifetime of a suspended moment in which to decide whether to block the punches or receive them. I chose to honor Fitzgerald's utterly incomprehensible pose of wronged virility. I took the love pats on my jaw and pretended they hurt me terribly. I even went so far as to sway sideways with the supposed momentum of the blows; and then, in the same fluid motion, I crumbled to a heap on the tiles.

Ham that he was, Mr. Fitzgerald brushed his palms together, satisfied with a job well done. By now, the bootblack attendant had rushed in from his stand in the vestibule. He looked at us, wide-eyed and open-mouthed, expecting an explanation.

"I TOOK THE LOVE PATS ON MY JAW AND PRETENDED THEY HURT ME TERRIBLY."

Still brushing his palms, Mr. Fitzgerald acknowledged him with a short nod. "That's that," Fitzgerald told the bootblack; and with that, he made his exit.

"Wait a second!" I called after him. "You owe me an explanation!"

He pretended he didn't hear me.

I am not well, Hyman. Writing to you made me forget about myself for awhile, but now I feel terrible again. I will explain later.

Henri

Dear Hyman,

After that escapade, I picked myself up and left the hotel. I
didn't want to make a scene. I was afraid that if I had re-entered
the ballroom, Mr. Fitzgerald's wrath might get the better of him
again, leading to further embarrassment and a compromising
of my subterfuge. It's not that I think the two of us can't be
seen together—but the less fuss, the better. The German spies
should not be aware of my dealings. So far, I sense I am being
regarded as a harmless speck of nothing sent to garner praise
for a little token country. The Germans will pay me no mind if
I play my cards right.

On my way back to the Garden of Allah, I grappled with
what had just happened. I had no idea why my presence had
inspired such fury in Mr. Fitzgerald. Perhaps Mr. Fitzgerald is
one of these Americans who loves France while despising the
French—whereas, we French despise both America and Americans alike. I understand that in all the time he spent in our
country, he never tried to pick up the language and he social-
ized exclusively with other American dilettantes—writers and
artists. I couldn't understand why he thought he recognized me.

It wasn't until later that night, after I'd returned to the hotel, that I realized we'd met before, at exactly the date and place he alleged.

1924 was a wild year. I was twenty-six, and one of the youngest successful architects in Paris, bidding on jobs against my mentor, Le Corbusier, and stealing some very big ones from him! My partner Phillipe and I had been in Nice on and off for the better part of a year, working on the plans for a glass hotel that was never built—though, at the time, we were optimistic. That summer I got together with three other fellows and rented an incredible villa. Besides me, there was Phillipe, my older brother Georges, and a friend of Georges' named Edouard Jozan, known to us as "Jozie". I was feeling my oats professionally at the time, mind you, but I was a church mouse in comparison to the rake I am now. It isn't that I didn't want every woman I laid eyes on, but with the Catholicity of my upbringing (my mother's Jewishness was a well-kept family secret), I got shy and tongue-tied. I tended to lose my train of thought every time I tried to put the make on somebody. Well, Georges' friend, Jozie, had never even dreamed of such problems. He was an inspiration to us all, and an opportunity for bawdy conquest seldom escaped us.

Jozie had some hot times with a few writers' wives. I met one of them when we were on the beach one afternoon. I don't think we were formally introduced—I don't remember getting her name (and I don't remember what she looked like, except for her bobbed hair). But she had a little girl with her. Now I realize that she must have been Fitzgerald's wife, Zelda, and her daughter Scottie. The little girl was two or three years old, and now she has just entered college. But I tell you, there were so many rich Americans all over the place at that time, it was impossible to know who they all were; and most of them said they were writers or painters or something like that. It never meant a thing to me. I'm not much of a literary "fan" or museum browser. I love the arts, of course, but I've never cared all that much about individual artists. I'm an advocate of the finished product, the work itself. If it inadvertently reveals a bit of its creator, well, that's okay. But if it draws too much attention to the puppeteer behind the curtain? Forget it, I'm not interested. I think Mr. Fitzgerald would agree, in theory at least. Still, as an artist himself he is boundlessly vain—which I hope will be to our benefit in what we are proposing to have him do.

So, all these years later, I guessed that Zelda Fitzgerald's affair was still very much alive—in her husband's mind, at least— and that Mr. Fitzgerald probably had mistaken me for Jozie, after having seen the two of us together. Jozie had a practice of meeting the husbands of his conquests. I seem to remember him joking about that—how absurd it was that he drank, played tennis, and went on picnics with the unsuspecting mates of the tantalizing Venuses he was simultaneously ravishing. Not that we French never fall prey to this sort of thing. But I remember we all thought the Americans were naive, even stupid, in being so blindly ingenuous and trusting with everyone they met. I suppose we were jealous of them, too, because they seemed so carefree and rich with hedonistic delight.

Mr. Fitzgerald had been affected. Maybe he hadn't shown it at the time, but the feeling had festered. He wasn't so carefree now. Very American, too, to try to keep the bad things down and let them build up—isn't it?

I decided to attempt to assuage Mr. Fitzgerald's present anger before it had time to rankle and fester even more. I changed my clothes, put on one of those V-neck college sweaters he likes to wear, and went to let him know I am not the man who slept with his wife.

There was night-blooming jasmine in his apartment building's otherwise unspectacular garden. I had never encountered such a fragrance before coming to California. It smells like candy. You can practically taste it as you breathe the air, and only at night—like the scent of a woman when you're in love. I inhaled it deeply and walked up the stairs to Fitzgerald's apartment.

He had a woman there—I should have known. I heard them arguing. It was the lovely gossip columnist Sheilah Graham who had broken from his embrace at the dinner dance. I stood near the door, away from the window, and listened. She yelled at him about the bottle she had found in his dresser; he yelled back that the bottle's contents were 100% water, and that it eased the pain of not taking a drink if he could pretend he was taking one.

"You're lying!" she screamed.

"Take it to a chemist and have it analyzed. There isn't one drop of alcohol in there!"

"I will!"

"Good!"

"If it's nothing, then pour it down the drain."

He must have emptied it, for their voices gradually softened to a whisper. After a brief interlude during which I heard nothing but a mosquito whispering sweet nothings in my ear, plaintive sounds wafted into the night air, and the perfume scent of the night-blooming jasmine rose to my nostrils from the yard below. They were both moaners. He made gruff, low cooing sounds, like a man-sized mourning dove. She made shrill little starts—a cross between a whippoorwill and a cute chimp. I swallowed.

My palms became moist. From my background information on the couple, I knew she would soon be dressed and out the back door. He and Sheilah never spent the night together. He couldn't because of his marriage to Zelda—he had to spare her delicate mind any added grief. Miss Graham had to keep clean or she might pick up something rare and incurable—the kind of ailment that comes from sorting through the stars' dirty laundry. They're after her and Louella and Hedda, her competitors. Personal scandal can be the death of a Hollywood gossip columnist, for the angry managers and studio gophers are always ready to return an old back stab.

Mr. Fitzgerald and Miss Graham's relationship is a public friendship and a private love affair. She is a divorcée, and he has been separated from his wife for at least five years. Everyone but Zelda knows about them. They've been lucky so far—Miss Graham hasn't offended anybody enough to inspire them to seek a gossip's revenge on the gossip.

Anyway—during this tryst, my only concern was that someone would see me from a neighboring building or the street. The porch light was out, fortunately. I crouched down, level with the wrought iron railing. Soon, I heard the back door open and close. Miss Graham's high heels clicked quietly, with well-practiced, confident steps, as she descended the wooden staircase on the backside of the building.

I waited a few more minutes, until I was sure she was gone. Then I knocked boldly. Soon, he opened the door a crack and peered out at me.

"Go fuck yourself," the great Fitzgerald said.

He tried to slam the door in my face, but I got my foot in just in time. "I am not Edouard Jozan," I said. "We shared a summer house togeth—"

"I don't care who you are." He kicked at my foot.

"Then why did you strike me?"

"I do not wish to speak to you."

"Jozan is a friend of my brother's. A bunch of us took a villa together that summer. Is this a crime?"

Fitzgerald pointed an accusing finger at me. "I remember your face. Zelda pointed you out on the beach. You had a nice physique. She said she was going to screw you after she finished with Jozan. And if she said she was going to, I'm sure she did."

"Is that my fault?"

"So, you admit it!"

"*Absolument* no!" I said, confused to be in this predicament. "I simply mean I am not responsible for what Mrs. Fitzgerald may have said. I have never touched your wife, I assure you, sir!"

"Bullshit, you lying frog!"

"You are the greatest living novelist. I recognized you and wanted to compliment you on your work. That is all."

"Thank you," he allowed, weakening briefly. "But that doesn't alter my opinion of you."

He was so certain of what had happened that part of me began to doubt my own memory. As I said, the two months with Jozie and the boys had been a wild time. A few girls were passed between us. One of us would take up where the other left off. Still, I think I would have remembered had I made love to Zelda Fitzgerald. Yes, she was beautiful at the time. She was also loud and eccentric. I don't remember carrying on with any loud, eccentric American women—only French, Germans, and Italians. There were a few Americans I liked, but they had been quiet and mousy. One I remember as being rather plump, if not obese. The other was so demure that she politely asked me if

I was "finished" once I had consummated the act with her—a
sweet frigidity (the sex was mental—she must have been doing
it to prove something to herself or somebody else).

Though, I did keep whatever doubts I may have to myself. It
is imperative that this man have no grudge against me and that
his suspicions be eliminated, or at least eased. If this could not
be accomplished, our mission would certainly fail —if not now,
perhaps later when I will require his loyalty.

"I am sorry you feel that way," I told him. "You see, I am
a writer myself—for the cinema. I had to come here when I
couldn't work in my own country any longer. I was hoping we
could talk. They speak so highly of you at my hotel—that you
are outgo—"

"Which hotel?"

"The Garden of Allah."

He brightened. After all, he had once lived in the Garden for
nearly a year, and many of his friends were still there. I thought
I had seen him walk through once or twice, en route to a bun-
galow, in the few weeks I've been here.

"Ordinarily, I would never have dreamed of approaching
you," I said, putting a humble foot forward once again.

"Why?"

"Because you are such a . . . giant of literature. Who am I to
speak to you? A stranger who has written a few failed foreign
films."

"They were made?"

"I'm sure you've never heard of them."

"What the hell," he said. "Come in and have a drink."

A truce, thank God, with encouraging overtones. I practically leapt into his apartment.

It was a drab green, but at least the building was new, and

the paint and furniture, too. There was nothing very homey about it, except for the nice little balcony off the living room. What we drank out there was not water, I can assure you. That was troubling—the last thing I wanted was to clink glasses with this incarnation of France's hope and watch him "fall off the wagon" (as the Americans call an alcoholic's failure to abstain), destroying himself before my very eyes. I brought up the problem as subtly as I could, and he assured me that we were drinking a diluted mixture (gin) that would not affect him "morbidly."

Before I knew it, Hyman, my friend, I could barely stand up. I looked out at the lights of the city below us, dancing about like something in a dream. I don't remember much, but I think I almost fell over the railing. I am not used to stronger liquors like gin and scotch and bourbon. They make one crazy. Maybe that's how we got to be in Mr. Fitzgerald's car headed for Tijuana.

I should not have let him talk me into it. But it was mad insane fun. He sang party songs in English, I sang them in French. We drove through fields of oil derricks. And then we were in a fog. I don't know how we didn't get killed. We lost our voices from so much yelling. I was so drunk I could not tell if it was truly a fog we were in or if the alcohol had induced a light gray haze. At some point, I think I demanded to know why it was taking so long to get to Tijuana, and why it was that Mr. Fitzgerald had decided we must go there.

"We are going to share the same woman," he said in solemn cadences.

"But I didn't do that with your wife," I somehow managed to summon up the presence of mind to insist.

"Regardless. We must have a Mexican Mary Magdalene. We shall sin and she shall forgive us, and by doing so we'll consecrate our pagan, sacred bond."

Or something like that. Whatever he said made me laugh so hard that I nearly wet my pants. I could not stop laughing until I was crying like an idiot.

I may have passed out for a bit because the next thing I knew, we were slowing down to cross the border. Hoards of dirty children accosted our car, bellowing at us in Spanish, and pounding their small fists upon the fenders and windows. After speaking to the Mexican crossing guard, Fitzgerald sped away, raising a cloudy shield of dust about us on the dirt avenue.

Thirty minutes later, we walked into a narrow bar lit by dim red light. Everybody looked like the devil with missing teeth. Paintings of bulls and matadors and plump, shawled virgins glittered and glowed in the reflection of a long, broken mirror above a stool-less bar where people were packed together like restless cattle. It smelled like cigar butts and urine. But I met an American blonde I liked there. She licked my ear and I touched her everywhere in a back booth.

Was I dreaming? The next thing I remember, I woke up. The sun glared in my eyes so that I couldn't see. Some invisible blacksmith was pounding my head over an anvil. I sat up, visoring my brow with both hands. Fitzgerald sat by a broken window, looking at me, smoking, and drinking a Coca-Cola. He was in the middle of the fierce shaft of sunlight, with his back to it, wearing skivvies. His pale neck glistened greasily and was reddened from over-exposure. We were in a large hotel room, it seemed. The floor was wood, painted black. There were bugs—big bugs—on the closest wall, going up the corner crack from the floor to the ceiling. Mr. Fitzgerald finished his coke, then opened another, using the heel of his hand against the window-sill.

"How about a Bromo?" he asked me.

He mixed it in an empty coke bottle and handed it to me.

"What happened?" I asked him.

Something growled beside me in the bed. I looked to the side and threw the covers off. It was the blonde I had dreamed of ravishing in the bar. She was beyond perfection—full-figured but undeniably firm. The sun woke her. She sat up, looking all the lovelier. A man never wants a woman more than when he is suffering the morning-after effects of too much drink. It works the poisons out.

I forgot about everything.

"Get your motherfucking hands offa me," she said when I touched her by way of greeting.

The young lady really did swear like a sailor. That was not surprising, considering she was married to one in San Diego—the ne'er-do-well type. She had come here for her share of trouble, and she had been ready for anything. It seems that the three of us had taken this room. I had become comatose on the floor, nearly expiring in a lumpy pool of my own vomit; Mr. Fitzgerald had lectured the would-be hussy on the perils of fleshly desire, the eternal sanctity of hearth and home and holy matrimony, until she became comatose herself—equally drunk and bored. She had the most beautiful legs, breasts, thighs, and eyes ("aquamarine" F. Scott Fitzgerald), and she said she hated both of us.

I had to watch her get dressed. She lingered over her silk stockings and brassiere, torturing me, and then stormed out of the room. And Mr. Fitzgerald thought it was amusing. It pleased him that she was so mad at us she was going home to her husband. But it didn't please me. I hate to get a hangover for nothing; and what made it hurt more was knowing how close and yet how far I was from being cured of this absurd agony. But she is gone, and for now my road-sore testicles have at least another hour to bounce in this jalopy before we are returned to Los Angeles.

Never again.

Your friend,
Henri

Hollywood
July 1, 1940

Dear Hyman,

On the way back to Los Angeles in the car, I discovered that Mr. Fitzgerald had been merely pretending to drink from his bottle. He either stopped the flow of liquor, tilting the bottle away before he swallowed, or expectorated the dangerous liquid when he thought I wasn't looking. He seems to possess a new-found respect for me now that he has seen me intoxicated. And despite my vicious hangover, I was pleased to witness his desire for self-control, however ambivalent. I am only afraid that I may have said something too revealing.

Could I possibly have "spilled the beans" (to use the American vernacular) and told him I am here to recruit him for the single most important political maneuver in the history of France (or the modern world, for that matter)? I doubt it. He wouldn't have been secretive about that—unless he had somehow decided I was a double agent (though I am, of course, it would seem). He would have barraged me with opinions, inquiries, and the like. Still, I'm concerned, for I have never been so drunk in my life. I suppose I did it because Mr. Fitzgerald appeared to enjoy it, and developing a strong, friendly rapport serves our long-range objective.

That is my only excuse. Otherwise, I am painfully ashamed. We are so fortunate we didn't have a fatal car wreck, driving in such fog and in such delirious spirits, whether inebriated or sober.

Once we'd arrived back in the city, Mr. Fitzgerald could not wait one extra second to check his mail (he was expecting $250 from a magazine for the recent sale of a short story). He turned at Laurel Avenue rather than continuing one block farther west on Sunset Boulevard to drop me off at my hotel. Ordinarily, I'd have been put off—especially in my road-weary, bone-tired, sod-headed condition. But considering the real and unspoken motives that had inspired my association with this man, I welcomed any excuse to extend our hard-won nascent friendship. Not that we were on shaky ground. It's just that the more time I spend with him, the more I will know him, the more he will trust in me, and the more easily we will be able to expedite our plans.

In any event, one doesn't want to appear conspicuous. After he parked the car in relative proximity to the curb, I did not invite myself in, but made a show of stretching, and then craned my neck about to remove the stubborn kinks as I stepped out of the car.

"I will talk to you soon," I said, pretending to wipe the sweat from my brow and waving as I turned toward the corner, letting myself limp slightly on my stiff legs.

He put an arm over my shoulder and steered me toward his apartment. "Come in and have a coke, for Chrissakes," he said.

To Mr. Fitzgerald's chagrin, his mailbox was empty. He peered suspiciously into the slots on either side of his own—annoyed that they'd received *their* mail. Then he made for his

stairs, taking them two at a time, tromping up rather purpose-
fully. I followed behind.

Mr. Fitzgerald's door opened before he had his key out of
his pocket. It was Miss Graham, with cold cream smeared over
her face and a Turkish towel draped over her hair in the style
of a turban. Apparently, she'd expected her love to be alone,
and began to close the door as soon as she saw me. She wasn't
wrong in being embarrassed, but once she realized the damage
was done, she opened it again, opting for an air of nonchalance,
pretending I wasn't even there. She began to lay into poor Fitzgerald —presuming, perhaps, that I was the bad influence that
had uncoupled her caboose from the shaky little engine and
train she had been foolish enough to buy a ticket to travel on.
She is a real task master—a royal monkey wrench which I'll
have to work around to get what we need here. She's not taking
any chances with her precious cargo, and she's not about to let
go of him for any reason. They have a deeply symbiotic relationship. It's hard to tell who's in charge, but I don't like her one bit.
It's not that she's mean or evil—but she's English, and they're
always stubborn in a small anachronistic way, if you know what
I mean. The English prefer to duel like sensible, high-minded
gentlemen, getting shot in the back while they're counting to
ten, rather than figuring out how to do things craftily in the
first place and win. They spent so much time coordinating their
battle plans with us, they forgot to do battle! The Germans had
all the time in the world to surround us.

But we must not dwell on the past. As far as the present,
Miss Graham bellowed at poor Mr. Fitzgerald. In her anger,
the pretty thing's sonorous English accent thickened to that of
a scrappy cockney scullery maid. Veins bulged in her neck. I

thought she was going to grab something and bang it on Fitz-gerald's head. She was certain he had been drinking and did not believe him when he protested otherwise.

Repeatedly, like an overprotective mother scolding her only child, she spoke of me in the third person: "I don't care what your friend does. If *he* wants to drink, well then, we'll let him drink. Let him expire in it if he wants to. That's *his* decision. You promised me, Scott. You promised!"

He kept trying to interrupt her, insisting that liquor had nothing to do with it. He said the two of us had been working all night on an idea we had for a film scenario. She didn't believe it for a second. She pointed out that Fitzgerald was caked with dirt—evidence of having driven long hours in the car.

Mr. Fitzgerald couldn't argue with her. He could barely squeeze a word in. He gave up, finally, changed his shirt, and then spotted the mail on a side table by the front door. He shuf-fled through it, frowning as if expecting the worst. But then he smiled like a child who had just been granted his most cherished wish. The check had come. He rushed back to the bedroom and returned a moment or so later, tying a jaunty blue-and-red polka-dot bowtie and carrying a blue blazer over his arm. He nodded toward his "Sheiloh," smiling ear to ear as she glared at him with her arms crossed hostilely over her terrycloth robe, doing her best to remind him that they had just been having a significant spat. Fitzgerald refused to let her interfere with his precious happiness.

"Where are you going now?" she demanded.

He came toward her, his brow narrowing, his smile turn-ing down a notch at the corners—a look of smug superiority. "Henry and I are going out for an early dinner. If anyone calls, take a message, baby."

Ms. Graham slammed the door so hard the draft practically knocked me off the stairs. Mr. Fitzgerald and I looked at each other and smiled like brother cats who had just eaten the canary. I don't know why it was so amusing, but it provoked a giddy feeling between us. As we strolled up toward Sunset Boulevard, Mr. Fitzgerald chuckled and I joined him. Men like to be bad boys at times. He was playing hooky from his responsibilities, he was free for a little while, without a care. I felt the same way myself until we passed a newsstand. NAZIS DROP FIERY BOMBS ON SCOTLAND, read the headline. ITALIAN AIR RAIDS KILL 145 IN FRANCE.

It's always a bit too much to comprehend, isn't it? How millions can be struggling for their lives while one is ogling leggy blondes and brunettes and trying to decide where to have dinner? This place is a narcotic. I do not know that I am ingesting it as the sun warms my skin, as the girls dance before my eyes, as the wonderful big band music tickles my ears—and within moments I am too much at ease. Then a vague doubt invades my pleasure of the moment and I remember who I am and what I am here for.

I seem to *want* to forget. Of course, I will not, but it's a normal reaction to such unimaginable chaos, don't you see? To dispute its existence at first, and then to simply forget it. How else can we live in the presence of such overwhelming death and disaster? People can only take so much. They have a hard enough time earning a living, satisfying their basic urges, and persisting with their dull daily routines. In general, no one has the time or peace of mind to worry about the welfare of those they do not know. This is our problem as Frenchmen and individuals.

We walked a half mile up to Hollywood Boulevard, then

turned east, passing a colorful gathering of movie cowboys, Union soldiers from the American Civil War, Indian squaws and braves (the latter's faces were streaked with turquoise and scarlet "war paint"), and two Indian chiefs wearing stunning peacock-feathered headdresses. About twenty of these actors filed off the back of a large flatbed truck, carrying trade magazines and wearing smoked eyeglasses (or "cheaters," as they are called) in the quiet of early evening, and shuffled off down the street together. A few cars honked their horns—tourists, according to Fitzgerald, though he hardly noticed them. This masked ball atmosphere is a business, he said. You get used to it. Farther on, he saw a couple of writers he knew. They were well-dressed but flabby, like the others I've met. They cursed their agents, and, with casual determination, name-dropped the assignments and producers they had recently survived or were presently anticipating.

I'm making light of this, but I should take it more seriously if I intend to impersonate this species of man. You see, writing for a living seems to be much different than any other profession. To do it well, one must be intelligent, to be sure—but the training is indeterminable. Some writers know many languages and have read all the classics in the original, in addition to being students of both the natural and physical sciences. Others are barely literate and work from imagination and experience. Thus, both the writer's constitution and his product are prone to subjectivity. Just as the learned practitioner of storytelling must constantly fret that he has forfeited his exposure to direct experience and cramped his imaginative faculties by steeping his mental apparatus overlong in the close moldy atmosphere of the cloistered study hall, so must the fast-talking, glib journalist fret that he lacks the requisite skill or wizardry of language to persuasively convey the natural disaster or domestic dispute he has just observed. It is a rare writer who combines knowledge with raw experience. I, for one, do not think it possible.

Your average scenario writer is forever doubting himself both as far as his ability and as to the merit of his labors. Doctors or lawyers or architects may doubt their abilities at times, of course—but a doctor never doubts his *existence* as a doctor. An architect never doubts he is an architect. Whereas, even in the brief time I have been here, more than once I have over-heard these writers discussing themselves or "kibitzing" (Yid-dish-American slang for "gossiping") about their friends, and they'll say, "Maybe I'm deluding myself to think I can make a living at this." Or, "He's got delusions of grandeur . . . If he's a writer, then I'm Pope Pius." I will not deny that I have gone through a major crisis of faith in my calling, but all I must do to resolve my collapsing confidence is design a structure and see it erected. I may still have my doubts as to its aesthetic quality, but if the building stands and is useful, I have acquitted myself professionally.

For the scenario writer, in contrast, so many other hands touch his work that often it is extremely difficult to determine his influence on the outcome. Critics and industry insiders often imply that a star or director "carries" a picture so that it succeeds *despite* the writing or the story. This leads the poor scenario writer to believe that his story or dialogue ruined the picture, or that it would have been better off with no story or writing at all. But how then would the picture have existed? These fellows never ask that question.

There is also the phenomenon of successes and failures. If the patient dies or the building collapses, the fault is not always with the surgeon or yours truly. But if a writer has a nice success with one picture which he follows with a box office failure, no one wants to hire him or even talk to him again. It is his fault. The picture failed because it was a bad script or story, and history is rewritten in regard to the previous success, which is retroactively attributed to factors unrelated to the writing.

This makes it very hard on the average scenario writer. It accounts, in large part, for his excessive drinking and general ill health. It also explains why most of the ones I've met are loudmouths. Each writer must be his own press agent and publicist, so to speak, to impress the studio "brass" that he's confident of his worth. It's as if he is presenting himself as a suit of clothes or a kitchen implement that will not be outmoded for some time.

After walking a few more blocks, we came into the dim, loud atmosphere of this well-known, plain restaurant[2] where Clark Gable or someone like him was supposedly discovered. I continued pursuing the topic of the scenario writer's plight with Fitzgerald. I cannot afford to parade my vast ignorance of the writer's lot. To shield my subterfuge, and as a means of establishing my credibility, I feigned a cultural comparison between the French scenario writer and the American, speculating that the French treat cinema as art, whereas America approaches cinema as commerce. Nervously rushing forward with a strident thesis that I was somewhat making up as I went along, I harangued Fitzgerald with the fictitious accomplishments of my alias—chronicling my collaborations on numerous obscure Cocteau and Renoir projects. It was quite absurd, really. F. wasn't listening very closely. He busied himself with a close

2. Duval is probably referring to the Musso & Frank Grill, a rather ordinary Hollywood bistro that has achieved legendary status by virtue of its long tenure among the ever-perishable establishments along the shabby promenade of ever-disappointing Hollywood Boulevard. (ed.)

study of the menu and impatiently waved in all directions for the waiter. As I talked of Renoir, he gazed about the restaurant, nodding agreeably. He was impressed initially, I think, with my confident air of seasoned authority. Then he became confused—he began to suspect I was discussing painting, not movies.

Mr. Fitzgerald knows little about French moviemaking—which is rather fortunate for me. It is difficult enough to be convincing in one's "true" self. The more people know us, the more they see beyond the surface and into our treacherous complexities, the less they trust us to be true. I think it is better not to know a man well, if you wish to trust him. I think this is why Mr. Fitzgerald has such a passion for storytelling and historical legends (and why, perhaps, my love is architecture). These things fuel a man's need to believe in something lasting and dependable—something knowable that exists with certainty and without contradiction.

But he wasn't inclined to argue the art versus commerce issue. The French are artists, and Americans are pigs, he readily agreed. He just wished he could make enough money to allow himself the independence of mind required to finish his new novel. He added that he'd have to bring himself up to date on French films; although, short of returning to France, he didn't know how he was going to be able to view them. He treats film—even something as banal as a Shirley Temple movie (a producer is trying to sign her to co-star in Fitzgerald's adaptation of one of his short stories)—as if it is a science. He acknowledges that films are execrable, frivolous products produced by callow, despicable, black-hearted men. But he treats the whole undertaking like it's a law of physics that one need only grasp in theory to benefit from in practice.

"I'm going to lick the picture game," he told me—the icy glint in his eye thawed by mischief, mirth, and a touch of joyful insanity.

I toasted us both, proposing the same aspirations for myself. We clinked glasses—mine a vinegary red wine, his a Coca-Cola.

We returned to the subject of France. "Why are you here," he asked, "when your country is at war?"

"As I believe I told you, sir, film production was shut down upon the German invasion."

"That goes without saying, but—"

"I fought in the front lines—infantry. We evacuated at Dunkirk, decamped in *Angleterre* with just a smattering of what remained of our division. You wouldn't expect me to return home to volunteer my services as a prisoner of war, would you?"

"But you could have stayed in England."

"*Pourquoi?*"

"To assist de Gaulle, of course, in carrying on the—"

"De Gaulle is a fool!" I forced myself to insist. "He is tilting at windmills made of giant razors that will lop off his head."

"But he will have lived his life for a reason, whereas you—"

"My dear friend, I have a wife and children to get money home to—to feed and clothe. What do you suppose will become of them without my support?"

"Somebody will take care of them."

"Easy for you to say."

"If everyone thought as you do, all of France might as well live in a cage."

"Bravo! You are so courageous, sir—perhaps you should join the Gaullists and the British yourself."

"If France were my homeland, buddy, I assure you I'd be the first in line to pick up my uniform."

"But France is a lost cause, I'm afraid."

"It's no wonder—if you're any indication of the average Frenchman."

I hid my joy behind the daily menu, knowing that Mr. Fitzgerald would presume he'd shamed me. I waited out a pregnant silence—"giving him the line," as his contemporary Ernest Hemingway might say, and encouraging him to plunge into deeper waters with the tasty hero's bait.

"I predicted it, you know," Fitzgerald bragged, puffing with a conqueror's pride at my imagined chastisement.

"How do you mean?"

"A little movie I wrote over two years ago—*The Three Comrades*. Monkey Wits—that's Joe Mankiewicz—changed the dialogue all around to ruin its effect. Nonetheless, it foreshadowed, predicted, and *condemned* the rise of Nazism. Unfortunately, its anti-Nazi sentiments were nearly censored out of existence due to the menacing lobby of the local German consulate."

I knew all of this already, of course, thanks to our exhaustive intelligence gathering. But for Mr. Fitzgerald's sake, I said, "*Mon dieu!* That is amazing."

"Not that it does us much good now."

"You can say that again—that's the American expression, yes? Though there is one thing—one very important thing—that could help matters for the French people. For all European peoples."

"I'm all ears."

"If America would enter the war."

His Irish face flushed—his chin becoming pronounced and pointy, emerging from its slack turtle folds as he glared across the table at me like a bulldog. "It's not our war," he insisted, his voice growing louder.

"To quote the poetry of your country's forebearers: 'No man is an—'"

"Don't give me that crock."

"What is a crock?"

"You're a lily-livered coward, and you want me to fight your war for you."

"The French are not and have never been cowards, monsieur. You *are* a coward."

He stood. I stood. We faced each other across the small table. The waiter had arrived at the table by now and looked alarmed as he stood there with his pencil poised over his small order pad. Patrons looked up from the booths and tables around us. We ignored them, engaged as we were in our incendiary argument.

"Your debt is personal, Mister Fitzgerald."

"Oh, it is, is it?"

"You would not have done any of your best work had you not once lived in Paris." I lowered my voice. "When the Americans join the French, then I will re-enter the fray with them. Until then, I will not hold my breath, as you would say. For I, at least—being a sane man of family—have enough sense to know I cannot walk upon water. I am not a martyr."

"That's for sure."

"You speak like a bully, monsieur."

The maître d' came over to separate us. "Gentlemen, lower your voices. Please sit down or finish this outside."

We stood our ground. "What you do not understand," Fitzgerald lectured me, as though speaking to an idiot, "is that by the time the US does enter this war—if that ever happens—it will be too late for you. The war will be over. Kaput."

"How long does it take a president to order his generals to be ready and disperse their troops?"

"Gentlemen," the maître d' said. "Enough. *Please!*"

I dropped a handful of change on the table. "This should more than cover the cost of that vinegar you Americans call wine."

I walked down the aisle toward the rear exit, as Fitzgerald catcalled after me. "Ah, why don't you go back to where you came from!"

I turned about. "Perhaps I will!"

I didn't wait for his response, but I believe the great Fitzgerald was surprised, and momentarily at a loss for words. He doesn't know what to make of me anymore, I'm sure. The only thing left for me at this point is to tell him. We have him right where we want him—you can see that, can't you, Hy? I'm just afraid of overwhelming him with the enormity of his role in this thing. And the last thing we can afford to do is to scare him off. We must proceed with caution.

That's what I keep telling myself.

Your friend,
Henri

P.S. I know these letters are an indulgence—a breach of the intelligence guidelines we set for operations procedures. Our code is a dilly, but not uncrackable, if anybody were to put his mind to it. We can't delude ourselves on this matter. I guess the reason that neither you nor I is really concerned is that no one is paying the slightest attention to France anymore. We're like the runt who has lost his way from a diseased litter. No one thinks we can either help or hurt. So, we feel we possess a sort of immunity from scrutiny. I hope we're right in being so complacent. Still, don't be cute—don't save this for posterity, my friend. It's one thing to take a letter from your P.O. box, and another entirely to stow it anywhere in your lodgings or somewhere else. Don't forget this, Hy. I know we've talked about it, but picture me putting a match to each of your letters over my bathroom sink as soon as I've read the last *salut*, and remember to do the same yourself—always!

Dear Hy,

The last few days have been gloriously hectic, coinciding with America's Bastille Day—or "Fourth of July," as they call it. Eager celebrants ignite fireworks day and night to commemorate the great occasion. To see them carry on with this pyromania, you'd think they invented gunpowder. I'm lucky I didn't get blown up. God knows my nerves are raw because of countless "cherry bombs" detonated in my path as I walked about doing my errands. In our line of work, there's always the distinct possibility that it's an actual bomb. I must confess that I was taken totally unaware once just after lunch at Schwab's Drugstore, when a carload of boys threw a handful of these toy grenades at me from their passing car. It was only after I had catapulted from the sidewalk into a large and bristly eugenia bush that my wits settled enough for me to see the amused faces. If these people knew who I was, perhaps they'd be a little more understanding. But what do they care?

Ugh! Let me stop before I sound like I'm feeling sorry for myself. I know what I'm doing here; though I may seem like a fool at times, I am not. If some people think of me as a naive or ignorant foreigner (which is the prevailing American attitude toward the rest of the world), so much the better. It's a bit humiliating to my male pride, I'll admit, but to be regarded this way is a useful camouflage. The other writers around the hotel think of me as someone who should wear a monocle—an artist manque who knows nothing about the nuts and bolts of writing a Hollywood movie. But that is all right. Every American I have spoken to knows so little about French cinema, I can say just about whatever I want and sound like an authority.

As a writer told me at the pool, "Let me give ya some advice, Frenchie. Forget the lighting and the fancy camera angles. Just remember: boy meets girl plus boy gets girl equals one helluva fuckin' commercial crowd-pleasing story. Keep it simple and you'll do just fine, kid." I had said I was looking for a job, you see. It frees the air between yourself and a stranger, to offer your definition of character right away so they know who you are and what you're looking for. And there's nothing one writer loves more than to give another writer advice.

Anyway, the morning after the altercation with F. at the restaurant on Hollywood Boulevard, I went for a run on the beach at Santa Monica. Then, after cooling off in the hotel pool (sans goldfish now), I wrote Mr. Fitzgerald a note, as follows:

Dear Scott,

    I have decided that you are right. I am the coward, not you! I shall rejoin my compatriots in the English trenches; perhaps if I submerge myself in the cause again with absolute dedication, I can make up for the time I have so shamelessly squandered here. Forgive me, please, as one who perhaps loves his country too much—as if it were a lapsed virgin, I suppose, whom—regardless of circumstance—one presumed foolishly, by a nonexistent

necessity, would always remain chaste. I have been in
shock at the loss of my one true love. I didn't think this
could happen to her. I ran from the truth; now I shall
return to salvage whatever remains of her fair virtue.
Thank you for waking me from my tormented sleep. You
are a clear-thinking man of rare courage, and a true
American. I know this is presumptuous, but if you have
a free evening in the next few days, would you do me the
honor of allowing me to host you to a quiet dinner at a
cafe of your choice? There are many things I would like
to discuss with you—one of which is the novel I have
been attempting to write.

Once again, forgive me. I said several ungracious
things I did not mean in my heart during our heated
discussion last night. You must understand I become a
madman when discussing France. And I have been
shouldering such a heavy burden of guilt and shame, of
which at last, thank God, I shall soon be free—thanks
to you.

It is my deep hope that I remain

Your friend,
Henri Duval

I know, Hy, that you're thinking I have boxed myself into a
corner—that I have no choice but to leave the country, whether
I enlist Fitzgerald or not. Yes, it was a chance, but we're dealing
with a theatrical personality in the great F. Scott—don't you
agree? He responds most favorably, with the best effect, to the
extreme—and it is an extreme situation, is it not? We *want* him
to be extreme, and to make a rightful, rash, and extreme judg-

ment of the world's plight. If we want to bring about extreme results, we must act extremely, too. I've decided this with calculation, mind you.

This is how it happened: I put on a robe of terrycloth over my swimsuit and slipped my new rubber sandals on. I dropped the note off at Mr. Fitzgerald's apartment, depositing it in his mailbox slot. Then I returned to the Garden pool, where I saw the lovely young woman who had unwittingly served as my muse while I sweated over my colorful prose composing the note I had just delivered. She was right where I left her, reclining on a lounge chair. As I walked around her, I thought I caught her smiling at me in the reflection of her three-sided tanning reflector.

I took another dip in the pool and came up on the side next to her lounge. It was a scenario tailor-made for me—no one else was there, except for a few dozing guests and occasional passing bellboys and chambermaids. But I couldn't get her eye—she was so absorbed in rubbing cocoa butter over her skin. Her face remained partly sequestered behind the shiny fortress as she spread the creamy fragrant lotion up and down her legs and thighs. She worked proudly, like an expert cabinetmaker oiling his newest creation. She lifted her legs with stiff elegance, and suddenly, as if she were about to launch into a reclining can-can. I know you have a wonderful wife and darling children, Hy, but I'm sure you remember these things. The thrilling scent of the hunt. You've got to know how I felt there in the beautiful clear air, the strong sun baking my neck and shoulders. Around me, redolent gardenias, hibiscus, birds of paradise, and gladiolas burst with color, as this huge human flower opened to me, with her indescribable hue, smelling of coconut cream, butter, and musk, her white-gold skin beaded in a fine sweat.

I concluded that she was determined to torture me with the fertile mystery of bodily delights swelling from that dazzling white elastic swimsuit. The short, wavy white-gold hair; her toasty, opalescent skin; the veins like lapis lazuli picking up deep sensual highlights from the tranquil, cool surface of the pool, reflecting the clear blue sky—all of her vibrated my soul like a tuning fork and conspired against the polite, reticent, settled demeanor I'd been trying so hard to cultivate.

But why? It is only natural that a married man, especially a purportedly married French man, should have an occasional affair. I have just been afraid to let myself get started here, really. There are so many women—bored and with nothing to do. They know they were designed for pleasure—giving and receiving—but they are afraid it is wrong to openly possess a nearly impersonal, beatific, and bestial urge. Their society creates institutionalized, large-scale superficial pleasures to channel their boredom into safer pursuits that won't malign their husbands. Markets here are transformed into huge aeroplane hangar arrangements called "supermarkets." Hardly anyone shops at a small self-contained boutique if they can help it. They buy at a department store, where they can purchase anything and everything under one roof in these monstrous hulking structures as big as Versailles. All to keep the little lady active and safe from sin with immoral opportunists like myself.

This one, though, was here for a purpose. She was "working the pool," as they say. No successful contract player would have had this much time to wallow away in. She looked the very definition of starlet (aimless, dumb, and sexy). I was willing to bank on it; otherwise, I wouldn't have felt so encouraged to be fresh with her. What is the worst that can happen in such a situation?

A haughty look? A slap on the cheek? I don't collect insults or relish acting like Tarzan of the Apes, but sometimes . . .

I pulled myself up out of the pool and sat on the lounge next to her. She remained entrenched behind her tanning reflector. I took the lotion from her hand and applied some to the ankle and calf closest to me. "I think you missed a spot," I said, pouring on my inimitably thick Maurice Chevalier accent.

"Gee, thanks bunches," she said, cracking her gum. She had a high-pitched Kewpie doll voice that sounded so phony it had to be real.

She turned toward me, with the three-sided tanning reflector still before her face, offering the front of her shins and thighs for my inspection. It was amazing. The only thing that tamed my ardor—ever so slightly—was her speech. I worked my hands over her legs while she prattled on, cracking her gum louder and making inane small talk. Her name is Ava Baker. Her father is a guard at Paramount Studios, where her mother works as a seamstress in the wardrobe department. She has met all the stars, from the earliest age. She nearly married one recently, though that is another story because she had been misled to think the scallywag was divorced.

She was indignant at the prospect of being a kept woman. "How could ya go on dates and stuff? I don't know what I'd do if I couldn't go out in public with a guy an' double date with one a' my girlfriends and her boyfriend. I don't care if he's Frank Sinatra—it's no fun 'less you can do stuff together. You know what I mean. It's the same way in France or any place in the world—wouldn't ya say?"

This is how she talks. When she got tired of holding the tanning contraption, she put a pair of opaque goggles over her eyes and lay there like a dead lizard. She sounded sincere as she continued gabbing this nonsense at an amazing speed, knitting her brows together and nodding smugly, as if it taxed her to think, for the sake of what I suppose she considered a stimulating, provocative conversation.

I don't remember exactly what I said, but I got her into my room with the outrageous request that she examine my wardrobe, to determine whether my suits were appropriately American. It went even more smoothly than I expected. I got as far as opening my closet. When I turned around with a double-breasted pinstripe model, she'd already stretched out naked on the bed.

"Let's pretend you're directing me in a scene from your new picture," she said longingly, sighing as she pronounced the last word, which seemed to take her breath away.

Somehow, she had gotten it into her head that I was a famous foreign film director. With my having been here just a couple of weeks, wouldn't you say it was too good to be true? The tryst was so easy and so fast that, frankly, Hy, it worried me a little. I had a girl like this five years ago. Mesmerized by her long legs and plunging neckline, I mistook her frantic daffiness for the latest in rarified cocktail wit. In less than a week, she had me climbing the walls. I used every excuse in the book but couldn't get rid of her. She pestered me night and day for months, sticking to me like glue. Finally, when I demanded that she leave me alone, she jumped out of my second-floor apartment window and broke her ankle. Then she brought me up on charges that I had pushed her. Luckily, she had done the same thing less than a year before with another admirer.

Now, in my Hollywood hotel room, I stood there, clenching the suit draped over my arm, keeping my passions to myself—but not without effort. "I would have given you such a line," I said, "but I never would have dreamed such a beautiful, bright young thing as yourself would believe it."

"What do you do?"

"I am a scenario writer, my love. Though if I were to direct, I must say you seem to radiate talent."

"I can see your radiator's overheated, too." She was tugging at my swimsuit.

"I just didn't want you to be disappointed."

"With this?"

"Thank you," I said. "Merci. Merci beaucoup."

She seemed to love it when I spoke French although it was obvious she didn't understand it, so I lovingly told her what an idiot I thought she was for spending her life lying by the hotel swimming pool. But the passion was an end in itself, and as we lay there in each other's arms, I couldn't help feeling that there was a certain admirable simplicity in the primitive mindlessness of it. I began to feel somewhat dandified—as if I had swept the sweet simpleton off her feet and overwhelmed her with my exotic male charm. I am handsome, I need to believe—more fit, I should say, than truly dashing. But the real reason she went for me, I'm afraid, is somewhat unflattering and rather circumstantial: I was there. The girl was numb from heartbreak with some other lover and anxious to flee her sorrows with the first bolt to come along (and I'm not even sure I was the first). She went through the motions of our lovemaking in tears, sobbing with a mixture of sad delight and grief, mumbling her apologies at first about how upset she still was about her famous intended fiancé. She had to let me know that she stood—er, lay—for something; in doing so, she evinced a heartening guilelessness. She was just too obvious emotionally to engineer the sorts of deceit I've encountered from the many damsels of my acquaintance in both low and high society. If anything, unconsciously, she's seeking revenge on her boyfriend, hoping to rub his nose in the painful, heartrending knowledge that he may have really missed something in passing her by. It made for a rather sweet abandonment. She performed quite boldly, acting like she was half out of her head—which I'm sure she was—calling me "Al" once or twice. (Capone? Ladd? Who knows?) I may have another lulu on my hands, but it was worth it. And it felt so good to lie against her when we were both spent and still.

Then, someone pounded at the door. We had fallen asleep for I don't know how long. Before I knew what was going on, a bellboy opened the door, and Fitzgerald and Sheilah entered, with a lady friend. The latter screamed with alarm upon seeing Ava and I sit up in bed. It was one of those shameless, ribald, outrageous, and theatrically absurd scenes that Mr. Fitzgerald is so fond of staging.

Not that I minded. He stood militarily erect and stiffly resplendent in a shining new tuxedo (a little too small for him), as he took in the salacious moment and watched our responses. A creative artist, this was his way—wryly observing and cataloguing his kindred species with studied pleasure; his eyes shifty, too, and narrowed, so zealously trained on the perceptual phenomena. Later, in the remove of thoughtful repose, everything he'd seen would become transformed (and transported) by his imaginative faculties.

Miss Graham and the other woman looked lovely in full formal gowns—lots of crepe, feathers, and tinsel, with long, white gloves; powdered, too, and more fragrant than I would have thought possible.

"I think we'd best leave," said the brunette stranger in an embarrassed panic.

Mr. Fitzgerald smiled. "Hello," he said calmly, as if we'd just run into each other on the street.

"Scott, please," Sheilah pleaded. "Your friend was . . . resting."

"Hi! How are ya?" said my babe in arms.

Mr. Fitzgerald turned to Miss Graham. "Sheiloh, *please*." Turning back to the bed on beat, he motioned to my strumpet with his cigarette holder. "Fine, thank you. We came to sing *his* praises." He smiled broadly with that long thin expressive mouth of his and signaled me with a humorous, repeated up and down beetling of his whitish-blond brows. "Your young warrior who has found his lost red badge of courage and shall return to inspire his countrymen in their emboldened leap into the savage fray."

He then proceeded to sing America's national anthem— "The Star-Spangled Banner"—which he has said was composed by a distant relative. For a moment, I wondered whether he had fallen off the wagon, but his hands were steady as he conducted himself.

As if to save Mr. Fitzgerald from embarrassment—if he's even capable of it!—Ava and the brunette joined in, singing quite boldly. Miss Graham is English, and so can be forgiven for remaining silent. Ava was still nude, with her full breasts exposed and jiggling. She looked lovely, I'll tell you.

Then Mr. Fitzgerald sang "La Marseillaise." He prodded me with his gaze, and though I resisted at first, I soon joined in. The two of us sang a duet, with Miss Graham struggling along. I put my foot down on "Mademoiselles de Armentieres," and then we were told to dress up in our best and meet them at the Trocadero in an hour.

As you may have guessed, I was more than a little concerned

about this new crimp in my plans. I was quite angry with myself
for having failed to properly anticipate Mr. Fitzgerald's response
to my letter. I should have been a step ahead—though perhaps
it's a godsend that I wasn't, because if I had been more cautious, I wouldn't have sent the letter in the first place, and nothing would have happened. I might have waited forever for the
proper moment to arise. My security was momentarily compro-
mised, but our fate—whatever it may be—in this mission will at
least not elude us for long. I could see that Mr. Fitzgerald fully
intended to sing my praises, as he'd said, to the world as a repa-
triated Free French Gaullist rebel. If the German underground
became privy to this, they could quite easily become suspicious
of my activities. What excuse could I give—that I was infiltrat-
ing the American left and suspected Fitzgerald might be a communist sympathizer I could use to my advantage? A possibility,
but a long shot.

I knew I had to nip this exhibitionistic mania of Fitzgerald's
in the bud before he exposed me. I knew I must confront him
with the full truth immediately.

I had a hard time getting rid of my starlet. I insisted that I
wasn't meeting Fitzgerald at all—that I had a previous engage-
ment for which I was already late, having been so delightfully
sidetracked and detained. She didn't go for it, but I got her off
my back by offering to suggest her for a major minor character
role. Cruel, of course, but what would you have done?

I called for the bellboy, had my new suit pressed (in the
heat of passion, it had been dreadfully smooshed on the bed),
and rushed over to the Trocadero, just a few doors away. I don't
know why, but I had unpacked my pistol and stowed it in the
inside pocket of my jacket.

Since it was still quite early, the restaurant was just starting to fill up. Mr. Fitzgerald and Miss Graham were at one of the best tables in the center of the room, drinking Coca-Colas in highball glasses as I know they do in lieu of cocktails. At the side of the table, by my place, was a stand with champagne waiting, corked and chilling, in its dignified silver bucket.

Mr. Fitzgerald and Miss Graham rose, smiling with proud glee at the touching and glorious celebration they were initiating. Their lady friend, who had been shocked at discovering me in my dalliance, was not there, thankfully (I later learned that she was intended as my blind date for this affair, much to her chagrin).

"Garçon." Mr. Fitzgerald raised his hand, snagging his upper arm in the tight jacket, but still snapping his fingers with embarrassing alacrity.

The waiter—a young, dark, handsome gangster-type—thought this was a joke being played for my benefit. He rushed over, bowed, and uncorked the bottle.

"Just one glass," Miss Graham said distinctly. "For him only."

Her nod indicated my position on the tablecloth.

He poured the champagne. I intuited the next move.

"Please do not make a toast to everyone present," I begged of both of them.

Miss Graham and Fitzgerald looked around. There were only fifteen souls, including the help, in the restaurant. Mr. Fitzgerald patted his smile off with his napkin. "My friend, a hero cannot be so shy."

"It is a special moment, Mister Fitzgerald. I would just prefer that it be shared quietly among us *only*."

Miss Graham misunderstood—though not really, I suppose. "Should I leave?" she said.

"No. No. That is not what I meant. My English sometimes leaves very much to be desired."

She smirked—disdainfully, I thought—and resumed her languor against the banquette. "Oh, then if you're sure you absolutely don't mind." She glowered at me, as if to say I was unworthy of such a distinctive display, and removed her gloves.

"Please, please. It is just . . . this is a very big decision for me."

I had no idea what to do. I stalled for time. For no sensible reason, within minutes, the restaurant started filling up with familiar-looking people—all of whom, in my paranoia, I suspected of being German spies. Then, looking utterly sensational in a faint silver evening dress that set off her fair skin and hair like klieg lights, my sweet strumpet Ava strolled past our table, glared at us, and continued to the bar.

Mr. Fitzgerald and Miss Graham wanted to know what the problem was—what had happened between us, and why I hadn't brought her along. Cryptically, I said we'd had a misunderstanding. Fitzgerald wanted to invite her to the table so we could make up.

"Not now. You see, I haven't told her."

"About your re-enlistment?"

"She's hurt. It was a casual affair, but still."

I felt I had to say that in deference to this insufferable romantic.

"With that time clock?" Miss Graham tapped the table with her furled gloves to emphasize a little titter that, for her, was a raucous belly laugh. "She's punched in and out with every pair of trousers 'tween here and Metro!"

"*Mon dieu,*" I said, trying to look shocked.

"Culture lag, Sheiloh," said Fitzgerald. "What does he know? The poor fellow's just been here a week or two . . . But I think you may have charmed her, Henry."

"You men," mused Sheilah, wrapping her arm around Fitzgerald's shoulders.

"I'll go and get her," said Fitzgerald. "Just you wait and see. I can get anybody to make up."

"You're a professional at it," offered Miss Graham.

"I suppose I am," Fitzgerald said, smiling. "I've had a lot of practice."

"No, please. This is not the right time," I said.

The man was like a mother hen. I couldn't put a stop to it. I slid out of the booth to restrain his impetuosity, but he locked his arm over my shoulder with firm fraternity and steered me toward the girl as I tried to veer away. "You're going back to France to fight for your country. No girl in her right mind can fail to comprehend the sacrifices of true valor."

He liked the sound and cadence of his voice, having strung together a good bit of blarney. He winked at me and waved ahead at Ava, who was making a show of pretending we weren't there.

"I cannot publicly announce I support and intend to defend the Free French cause."

Fitzgerald looked at me like I was mad. "Why not? It's a free country, isn't it? Or, it should be."

"Please. I simply cannot."

"You're a patriot, fella. Wise up and be proud of it." He tapped a passing patron on the shoulder. "You look like an intelligent, unbiased third party."

"Excuse me," said the stranger.

"I'd like to solicit your opinion, if I may."

"Please, Scott," I said.

But Fitzgerald went on: "This Frenchman has recovered from the shell shock of the triumphant evacuation at Dunkirk. He is returning to the cause. Should we or should we not toast him?"

The man turned to me. He was a big burly character-actor type—like a shaved bear in a dark double-breasted suit that looked like it would pop its buttons if he took a deep breath from his barrel chest. His mouth had that crooked gangster leer which seems to be a mandatory expression for all virile males here. He nodded. "Fuckin' krauts," he bellowed in our faces, spraying us with the residue of bourbon that had been on his upper lip. "Buy him a drink."

"See. What did I tell you?" Fitzgerald patted me on the back.

The friendly patron tipped his highball at us and walked away.

I slipped out of Fitzgerald's clutches. "I must talk to you," I said. "Now."

Mr. Fitzgerald looked concerned. "Why, sure."

We made our way to the restroom and entered. "We've got to stop meeting like this," Fitzgerald said jauntily. I barely heard him, as I was checking the facility for eavesdroppers. "It can't be that bad," he went on. "An hour ago, you were in each other's arms. A man gets lonely—you can't help it, especially in these times."

I turned to him after checking the last toilet stall. "It's not the girl. Listen closely before we are interrupted. Yes?"

"I'll tell you one thing, Henry. I know I'm only a year or two older than you, but—"

"*Please.* This is not the time."

"It's possible to have high purposes without being so solemn."

A man had come in to relieve himself, so I was forced to listen to this advice to the lovelorn until he left. "You must not discuss my re-enlistment," I said, when the stranger was gone.

"Why not?"

"I know America is a free country. But Europe is not."

"But you're not in Europe, are you?"

"I have cultivated your acquaintance for a reason, Mister Fitzgerald, and I cannot let you ruin it."

Fitzgerald looked confused and somewhat alarmed. "What are you talking about?"

I stared him down angrily, fixing my eyes on his, demanding with my vise-like gaze that he hear me out in utmost seriousness. "I am a spy, Scott. I never abandoned the cause. I am the founder of L'Esprit Libre—a militant group working in secret resistance to the Vichy regime."

"But you said you—"

"Forget everything I said. I was setting you up, as your gangster movie heroes would say. It's true—and it's also true that I have come to recruit you for what may well be the most important single mission to secure the fate of the world. I am here to give you the supreme opportunity to rewrite history without lifting a pen—if you will only commit yourself to our cause for a free France and free Europe."

"I'll commit myself to the nearest sanitarium if I get any closer to your breath!" Fitzgerald sniffed at me, thinking that perhaps I had been slyly indulging in alcohol.

"No. I have not been drinking."

"Well, it's a good joke." He slapped me on the back. "Do you have an extra secret decoder ring?"

Quickly, with cold, uncalculated necessity, I extracted the pistol from the inside pocket of my coat, and placed the barrel against the great Fitzgerald's head. "These are not blank charges," I said. "I am serious."

Fitzgerald looked terrified, somewhat like one would imagine he would look if the devil incarnate appeared out of nowhere by the side of his bed in the middle of the night and shook him awake with coal-hot skeletal fingers. "What do you want from me?"

"I cannot tell you here in a rush. This much I will say: I have sought you out personally. You are the only reason I have come to this country, sir."

"But why?" His voice rose like that of an inquisitive frightened child.

"You are going to help France and her allies win the war. I do not wish to make you nervous, but everything depends on you. You are the most important free citizen in the modern world!"

He produced a nervous fake smile, looking as if he now had the situation figured out. "This is a practical joke. You must be a friend of Ernest's."

"Ernest who?"

"You know who I mean."

"Only because I have done such exhaustive intelligence on you."

"I EXTRACTED THE PISTOL ... AND PLACED THE
BARREL AGAINST THE GREAT FITZGERALD'S HEAD."

"Including reading my work?"

"Yes. I have read everything."

"Name some titles then."

"Not now—though I will say *The Great Gatsby* and your recent pieces are my favorites."

"It's out of print." He stepped back, pulling his head away from the barrel of the pistol. "Could you please remove the gun?"

I put the pistol back inside my coat. "I am giving you the opportunity to have the world rediscover who you are, sir, as a world-class celebrity . . . or, if you will, a humanitarian on the order of Saint Francis . . . or, if you aspire only to literary stardom, a classic modern novelist. Whatever your heart's desire, you shall have it, if you deign to honor our cause, whether you live to tell your story or not."

"Who is this mission for?"

"The free world, sir."

"The Free French—de Gaulle's men?"

"Yes."

"America supports you. What are you being so damn-it-all frightened and secretive about?"

"I am a double agent. I work for Pétain's gang, but I have pledged my true soul's fullest loyalty to Charles de Gaulle. I am the Assistant Minister of Foreign Affairs in the new restructured French-German government. Monsieur Pétain believes I am recruiting you to help oil France's new propaganda machine."

"Why?"

"Why does France need propaganda? To impress the Germans, of course—so they think we French want nothing more than to subordinate ourselves to Germany and peacefully co-exist with them for the good of France."

"No."

"It hurts to say this, even, but yes, it is true."

"And what am I supposed to do about it?"

"Pétain is one of your fondest admirers. He wanted to be a famous author himself."[3]

"So?"

"You are going to befriend Pétain."

"For what purpose?"

"What do you think?"

"I don't have the foggiest idea. What could the Free French forces possibly want with a washed-up tubercular old rummy?" He seemed almost proud of his fragile Keatsian condition.

"So that you can kill him," I said.

He fainted straight away, dropping limply into my arms.

3. "The Marshall not only had literary friends, he also had literary aspirations." Richard Griffiths, *Pétain* (Doubleday, 1972), 94.

Hi Hy,

Sorry I didn't finish yesterday—I had to take a nap. I have been going nonstop, as I will attempt to explain; besides, there is only so much one can write in one sitting. My hand cramps. After scribbling on for hours—culminating in a pleasant delusion during which I feel giddily inspired as I turn what I think is a nice phrase or two in describing recent events—I begin to lose my bodily sensations: the hind end and spine turn numb, the limbs useless, achy and stiff, leaving me light-headed and yet more inert, somewhat like an overripe pear or tomato past its prime. I keep telling myself what good practice this writing to you is, even though I know it's like sky-writing or writing in the wet sand close to the shoreline of the sea. By the time I reach the end of a sentence, the beginning of it has disappeared.

And the writing practice is good for me, I know, for I have lost not a little sleep while fretting over the horrors I might encounter if I am "found out"—i.e., if I am called upon to actually write something and can't. I guess, in a sense, I am beginning to think as if I were a writer, even though I am not. The professional writer, I am sure, must feel the same way.

I may have said this, but it is strange to compare the head-splitting work of creating a building on paper and writing a story. When I have completed the plans to a home, hotel, or office building, I know it. The result, as constructed, may look slightly different than what I have envisioned, but it will never shock me or my client as being antithetical to or jarringly different from what I intended. Such, I understand, is not the ordinary process with the arts. Think of all the music, books, paintings, and sculpture filling the libraries, museums, and culture centers of this world. Most of it is indisputably terrible, even in its time and for the audience it was intended to edify or elevate. At least as far as writing is concerned, that may be because of the myriad (and maddening) significations of words, words, words. For their author, they say one thing and spring so majestically and unequivocally to life; for the patient, harried, or tired reader, it is another story altogether, or perhaps no story at all. There is absolutely no guarantee that the writer will be able to recreate in the mind of anyone else the precious something he has discovered for himself. Yet he wants to.

It's a bit ugly, this desire to possess another's mind with one's own thinking—gods, demons, and all. Storytellers are creeps, in a way. No wonder they have so many problems. The only way they can succeed is by dominating a large audience with their personalities. This sounds suspiciously close to how one would define a priest or politician—wouldn't you say?

After reviving Mr. Fitzgerald with damp hand towels, and then getting him to take a few deep breaths and wash up at the sink, as I directed him back through the dining room, supporting him gently under one arm, I had told him he could not, under any circumstances, confide a single word of what we had discussed to Miss Graham.

Heads turned, as many eyes had followed Mr. Fitzgerald's

shaky progress through the restaurant as we navigated between the tables looking for our own table. It was obvious he was very unwell. You would have had to be blind not to bear some witness to the precarious predicament he now found himself in which, nonetheless, shall remain mysterious and inexplicable to all concerned here (except you and me and Mr. Fitzgerald), including Miss Graham.

Anyway, when Mr. Fitzgerald and I returned to Miss Graham at the table, her fair face was taut with anger, and her bright eyes had glazed over with inward absorption, as we had given her a rude bounty of seemingly endless minutes to rehearse chastising speeches for our having abandoned her. Her lips were pressed tightly together for composure and restraint.

"Thank you both for the insult. You left me sitting here for so long I'm surprised I'm not all covered in moss. If you don't mind, Scott, you might spare me any more embarrassment if you could somehow find it in yourself to tear yourself away from your very new best friend here and escort me back—"

She stopped herself as she noticed the state Mr. Fitzgerald was in—white as a sheet, his limbs and posture rigid with the shock of what had just transpired between us in the toilet. He looked like he was about to fall right over the table and booth like a felled timber.

"Darling, what's wrong? You look as if you've seen a ghost!"

"He fainted," I explained to her. "Very briefly, but I suggested he stay still until the dizziness passed."

"I'm sorry, Sheiloh. Something came over me. I don't know what happened."

"You shouldn't skip lunch," she scolded, tenderly. "Haven't I told you?"

She got up and took Fitzgerald by his free arm. We set him

down in the booth. He looked around to see if anyone had noticed, and the gaping hordes glanced quickly away. The noise level returned to a normal volume.

"I know," Fitzgerald said. Miss Graham framed his face with her small hands and looked up into his nearly blank eyes with the adoring, penitent concern of one being appropriately self-critical for having jumped to the wrong conclusion. You could see they loved each other—they were both so decorously demonstrative about it. Frankly it made me a little queasy. I know it shouldn't have. It's just that they poured it on so thick, and yet with such propriety-minded restraint, I could hardly believe that such chivalrous gentility could coexist with the youthful ardor of the depthless "true" love that authors like Mr. Fitzgerald and his romantic predecessors are so fond of depicting. But their circumstances are special and complex, and I'm exceedingly cynical. And how would anybody react to seeing their loved one walk into the room looking like death warmed over? They would be numb with shock, just as Miss Graham was.

I sat there and waited patiently while they made goo-goo eyes with each other, and Miss Graham continued to softly chastise F. for his poor eating and health habits—not enough fresh air or nightly rest.

"But that's your fault," Fitzgerald cooed, and then he started coughing terribly (he has an awful hack, which may be the result of his strong dependence on tobacco). He clutched his chest. I took his cigarette from his hand and extinguished it immediately—as if one act could remedy this poor physical specimen's shameful decrepitude.

"I think Mister Fitzgerald should rest," I told Miss Graham.

She retrieved her fur, and we made a hasty retreat. Mr. Fitzgerald felt too weak to walk the short distance back to his apartment, so we had the doorman call a taxi for us. I'm telling you, Hyman, my palms were so clammy they were crawling. I was so afraid of what Fitzgerald might confide to Miss Graham once the two of them had dropped me off at the Garden of Allah. I could not let Fitzgerald out of my sight until we had the opportunity to further discuss the situation. Any leak in security could mean the demise of the Pétain operation—and my head, too, if word of our scheme were to reach the authorities.

I didn't know what I was going to do until the taxi pulled up before the hotel and I saw a small gathering of photographers waiting with their flash cameras for some celebrity to come out of the Garden.

I leaned back inside the taxi after exiting. "Miss Graham, excuse me."

"Yes, Mister Duval." Pressed lips; very impatient.

"I am not certain this means anything to you, but I forgot to mention that I met Errol Flynn this morning at the pool."

"How interesting. May we discuss this at another time, perhaps? Scott should be getting home."

"Of course. He invited us—I told him about you both—for cocktails. A nightcap, I think you call it—after dinner."

"I could use a piece on him. Maybe some other night if he's available."

I locked eyes with Fitzgerald, urging him to encourage her, but to no avail.

"He said he would like to meet you—purely professional. If he's going to be written about, he'd rather be written about by someone fair, I think is what he told me. But he will talk with you some other time, perhaps."

"Yes, of course." She looked flustered, glancing askance at Fitzgerald, as if to confirm that his condition was still alarming.

"How do you feel, darling?"

"Sound," Fitzgerald answered in a meek but angry voice.

"I have an idea," I enthused. "It would be a shame for you to miss what they call an exclusive, Miss Graham. Mr. Fitzgerald will be fine with me—won't you, sir?"

He nodded, finally, getting my intent.

"I will see him up to his apartment, and we will see you in what—half an hour?"

"Wait a minute." Fitzgerald was rallying, so it seemed—unfortunately. His puffy face colored as he recovered from his slumped posture and pulled himself erect to glower downward at Miss Graham. "You'd rather gossip with this . . . buccaneer than make sure I'm okay. Is that it?"

Miss Graham straightened Fitzgerald's tuxedo collar and smoothed her hands down his satin lapels. "So, it's gossip tonight, eh? Yesterday, you allowed that my line of work was capable of real dignity, along the lines of the diaries of Samuel Pepys. I can see you're feeling better—you're acting jealous."

"I'm calling you at his room."

"We're not going to be in his room, silly. I'll page him, and we'll be at that dingy bar in the hotel. You're welcome to join us."

"I met him before. Who wants to listen to a boring actor talk about all the dumb things he's looking forward to in his next picture?"

She got out of the car, thank God. "Then I shall see you in a short while. Thank you, Mister Duval."

"My pleasure." I latched onto her hand and kissed it, assuming she'd appreciate the gesture. She thanked me, but F. frowned. "Keep your lips to yourself," he said, eerily expressionless. The elderly cab driver turned around to see if he was missing anything. The great Fitzgerald laughed throatily before tapering off into his usual smoker's cough.

I got back in the taxi. As we pulled away from the curb, and Miss Graham waved, Fitzgerald continued baiting her: "Ask him what he eats for breakfast—who his tailor is. Don't forget to discuss Plato and the Greeks! Sophocles, Euripides, Aeschylus, of course—he's very intellectual. He'll want to try Shakespeare after he finishes supervising the building of his new house!"

F. lost this buoyant sarcasm a few minutes later when we arrived at his apartment building. I forget what the fare was—a franc or two—but Fitzgerald thought it excessive and made a terrible scene and wouldn't allow me to pay the driver, a poor old little fellow with unwashed white hair, wearing a filthy tan suit so pitifully big on him that the frayed sleeves covered all but his yellowed fingertips. He had the shakes, too, even before Mr. Fitzgerald berated him.

The cab driver was quite surprised at first, as Fitzgerald insisted the best way to resolve a disputed dishonest charge was to not pay it at all.

The old fellow sat there, staring straight ahead through the windshield of his sedan, ignoring Fitzgerald's pointed remarks, even though Mr. Fitzgerald became incensed, pugnaciously leaning forward to holler in the little man's ear. Then he took me by the shoulder and directed me away. "Let's go."

No sooner had we ascended the stairs, entered Fitzgerald's apartment, and turned on the lights than there was a series of light knocks at the door. Mr. Fitzgerald opened it.

"You better pay," said the taxi driver, his chin jutting forward so that the comb of loose skin wobbled down his throat.

Mr. Fitzgerald swore at him like a schoolboy and slammed

the door—all of this over a mere franc. The little man kept knocking.

I laughed. It was absurdly funny, and I kept expecting Mr. Fitzgerald to pay him so he'd go away. But Fitzgerald wouldn't. We stood there, staring at the closed door. I made numerous attempts to resolve the matter myself, but Mr. Fitzgerald held me back each time.

"This is ridiculous," I told him.

"It's the principle," Fitzgeald said. "I don't care if he is seventy-five."

"Fine, then. We'll let him die on your doorstep from overexertion."

"He didn't even apologize for fleecing us. Try to imagine, if you will, all the others he's fleeced and will continue to fleece— all the corners cut, and unscrupulous actions performed. I won't have it on my conscience, letting anyone get away with something like that."

I was determined to turn this single-minded obstinacy masquerading as idealism, to the purpose at hand. "Good," I enthused, as the feeble old guy kept tapping away. "Good. Then you must feel the same way regarding France and the European continent."

"I do!"

"But you turn one cheek, and the Nazis come to power; turn the other, and the free world, as we know it, will be gone!"

The pitiful two-fisted pounding was weakening. I could hear the little old taxi driver wheezing through the door. Finally, I could stand it no longer. I pushed Mr. Fitzgerald aside and swung the door open. The little man stood there, his fists clenched, his back stooped and head bowed, somewhat like an ancient snapping turtle with dentures. He snapped up the five-dollar bill I held out to him, grumbled something about calling the police next time, and took his leave.

"What are you doing!" Mr. Fitzgerald screamed at me.

A few of his curious neighbors had peeked out to see what was going on. I nodded politely and closed the door. "An idea or principle is never more important than a human being," I told him.

"But he lied!" Fitzgerald whined. "He took a circuitous route for no other purpose than to pad the fare!"

"Is it possible to be an honest capitalist? I think not—unless you can afford the luxury."

"Are you a communist, too?" asked Fitzgerald.

"No, no, no. I am a realist. Man is a competitive beast capable of occasional kindness. The taxi driver is just a poor tired old man doing the best he can to make a living. Sometimes he's honest, sometimes he's not."

"You're advocating amorality."

"I am advocating compassion—'negative capability,' as your favorite poet John Keats espoused. We must be able and willing to put ourselves into the shoes of others to gauge how they feel and think."

"Take your own advice then."

"How so?"

"Well . . ." He rubbed his chin, a mischievous glint in his eye. "Put yourself in Pétain's place . He means well. I'm sure he wouldn't appreciate being killed."

"And neither would Hitler. I merge my soul with the feelings of *real* men and women—common, regular people—not aberrant egomaniacs who look upon the world as their oyster, with no concern for the lives of anyone else. Thousands of people are dying. Don't you understand?"

"What are *you* doing to stop it?" demanded Fitzgerald

"I am here recruiting you."

"To kill Pétain? If he's such a monster, how come you're so chummy with him?"

"I am not chummy, as you say. I happen to have helped design a home for him," I lied. "You see, I am really an architect, by profession. My English is passable, and I have catered to the wealthy American expatriate trade. Knowing this, Marshal Pétain offered me a cabinet post as Assistant Minister of Foreign Affairs, after we became friendly. Also, I urge you to remember that the Marshal was until quite recently a tremendous hero, a legendary patriot of the Great War. He simply became too full of himself, ruining us militarily, with his antiquated strategies, and ignominiously dumping the most civilized nation into the maw of these German cannibals—just to save his own pampered skin."

"But how will killing him solve any of France's problems?"

"Don't you see? An *American* kills the puppet premier of France?"

"One puppet can always be replaced with another."

"Yes, yes, of course, but first the Nazis will condemn America as the world's most vicious, blood-mongering imperialist threat, and war will be declared against you."

"Great," sighed the confused Fitzgerald.

"Great, indeed, my friend—for the sooner America lends a helping hand, the greater chance freedom has to survive."

"FDR will deny any connection with me."

"And Germany will refuse to believe him."

"What you're saying is that you and your resistance group want to use me as a catalyst to spark America's forced entry into your war."

"*Our* war."

"Our war, your war. This is the craziest thing I've ever heard. You must have just escaped from an insane asylum."

I showed him my official documentation, including the letters of introduction from Laval and Pétain. I told him of the scheme which would ultimately involve the fiction of Fitzgerald doing a *Life* Magazine piece on the old fool. The first step is to assist Fitzgerald in establishing a correspondence with Pétain— who owns personal translations of all of Fitzgerald's published works, who prides himself in his knowledge of contemporary American literature, and who, thankfully, is oblivious to the fact that Ernest Hemingway is both a more commercially successful and a more respected writer presently in America. Mister Hemingway's current earnings far eclipse Mister Fitzgerald's; what's more, Hemingway has become somewhat of a living legend in this country. It goes without saying that Mr. Fitzgerald is painfully sensitive to this fact, and I heaped salt on his wounded psyche by reminding him of it. Did Mr. Fitzgerald really believe that Hemingway had no ulterior motive in traipsing about the continent to "report" on the war? Why shouldn't Mr. Fitzgerald come out of hiding to do the same thing?

"To go on a suicide mission?" he asked. "I think not."

He paused. I knew I had him, and so I went for the jugular: "How much longer are you willing to let that bully overshadow you? Here you have an opportunity for a humanitarian commitment that will serve a greater purpose while glorifying your artistic ego at the same time—and you're going to let it pass you by? Shame on you! It's not every man who has a chance to realize his own apotheosis . . . don't forget your books are nearly out of print."

"I don't want to die."

"Who does! But death in this mission is not a foregone conclusion."

He smirked. "That's reassuring."

"Every effort will be made to ensure your safety—and my own. I want to live, too, you know. So does the rest of Europe."

"You'll be with me?"

"Yes, of course," I assured him. Though, between the two of us, Hy, who knows? I may well lose my life here in Hollywood first.

"I still don't understand," F. offered at last—hedging further, I thought, in committing himself for once in his life. "You're going to write Pétain, saying you've met me. Then you think the premier of France is going to write me a fan letter?"

"Yes."

"And then I write him back. After a couple months of this, I offer to do a piece on him for *Life* magazine—without telling *Life*—and he eagerly accepts my offer and extends an invitation to me to come interview and observe him."

"Especially after I've assured him—in my official correspondence—that you're sympathetic to the Axis cause."

"No."

"I'm afraid so. He loves your writing, but what good are you to him if you can't help him feed the Nazis what they want to hear . . . The fate of nations is at stake, man!"

Too sententious a pronouncement, perhaps, for Fitzgerald once again began to look rather piqued. He excused himself for what seemed like a long time. I heard a great deal of clattering, as if he were looking for something in the closets. Then, it was too quiet.

"Mister Fitzgerald?"

I found him in his bedroom, standing rather precariously on top of his dresser, a pint flask of a crystalline elixir pressed, or rather glued, to his lips. A storage cabinet, where he had stowed his emergency relief bottle, was open just above his head. I could see that he had just begun imbibing, as the bottle was still full—but in a moment or so, it would be empty.

"No, sir, no," I barked, startling the guilty beast, who promptly lost his footing, careening backwards into my waiting arms. The bottle sailed over my head, landing against the side wall to the left of the bedroom door, and draining onto the floor.

Stunned, Fitzgerald stepped away from me, then stood still. Tears came to his eyes—then he was sobbing, on his knees, retrieving that godforsaken crutch of his and puckering up to it again. I grabbed it from him and, with a dramatic flourish, cast the evil thing out the back window. We heard it break on the asphalt in the rear alley, with a crash that made a popping sound as the glass made a small explosion upon impact.

It was an eerie moment I shall always remember.

The two of us glared at each other: Fitzgerald's slightly bloated mask of maudlin shame; mine, I suppose, maniacally grim and savagely stoic. "You must be strong," I urged this ruined wreck of genius. "You must be clean to be of any value. Your mind and senses must be the keenest—honed to the sharpest point they have ever been. You must model yourself after a prizefighter on the comeback trail, if we are to have any chance of surviving what we are going to do."

"I can't, Henry," he chanted over and over. "I can't."

I couldn't stand his defeatism, Hy. As you can guess, we

came to blows. I slapped him with the flat of my hand. He tack-led me—as they are wont to do in that primitive, bastardized version of football only Americans could love.

A lady's heels clattered up the stairs. Miss Graham was returning. We froze.

"It's Sheilah," Mr. Fitzgerald announced.

"Yes."

We got to our feet. I hurried through the apartment, making haste toward the service stairs in the kitchen. I didn't want to wait for Miss Graham's wrath, as I knew she would be very angry with me.

"Don't disappoint me," I called back to Fitzgerald. "A truly great writer can only be so if he is also a great man. Your best work awaits you if you decide you are equal to the task."

"I'm so sorry, Henry. I *can't* do it."

"But you—"

The front door opened. I slipped out the back.

"That bastard creep frog," fumed the raging gentlewoman. "Errol Flynn left yesterday!"

Hy,

I slept for just a few hours, waking before dawn. I was anxious about Mr. Fitzgerald. I sat and stewed, cursing myself for having been precipitous in broaching things with him. His nerves are so frayed normally that he crumbles at even the simplest tasks, such as keeping his car up, taking care of his laundry, having his manuscripts typed, and such. I clearly overwhelmed him.

But there was no other way. The appropriate moment for such bold tidings does not exist. Even Kubla Khan would blanch, knees quivering at such a challenge. Maybe it cannot be done, at least not by F. Scott Fitzgerald. Whatever made us believe he would be equal to the task? If Pétain weren't such a nostalgic imbecile for the Roaring Twenties, we could have gone with Hemingway. He once would have jumped at this opportunity—though who knows whether he'd still be hungry enough to take the terrible risk today. He may believe, however falsely, that he has already transmogrified himself into immortal clay. Why would he gamble it all on the undecided chimera of the mere fate of our drab and very mortal world? After all, literature is history's whore—both beneath and above it all and getting the short end of the stick whether she plays the gutter tramp or haughty queen. If Hemingway were to stand up for what turned out to be a dying cause—if the Nazis revise our cultural inheritance—it could look bad for his coveted spot in the literary pantheon.

A Nazi world, a Nazi future. I shudder to commit the words to paper, or even to think it. I was thinking about it, though, and shuddering, when footsteps sounded on the walk outside, then shuffled up my stairs. A brisk knock tattooed against the door.

It was Mr. Fitzgerald, of course, still wearing the same tuxedo from the previous evening, without the jacket, but with the tie still knotted and his sleeves loose, having removed or shaken off his cuff studs. His hair was on end. He looked pale—just horrible. I feared he'd been drinking.

"I couldn't sleep," he said.

"Why?"

He extinguished his cigarette on the top step and extended his hand. "I am at your service," he said quite softly, his normally husky voice overwhelmed with the humbling spirit of a moment larger than he had anticipated.

I grasped his hand with my own. "I am not shocked," I said, "though I am certainly surprised—pleasantly, of course."

I ushered him inside, closed the door, and hugged him like a brother.

"*Vive la France!*" we both said. I needn't tell you—there were tears in our eyes.

After we caught our breath, Fitzgerald wanted to go over the plans, and review (and revise) strategy. But I felt we were both overwrought with sheer excitement stemming from the exhaustive process of research, pursuit, discovery, and deliberation, culminating in that fiery decisive moment of commitment to the cause. In other words, I convinced Mr. Fitzgerald that it would be best to wait out our excitement a bit—to let it settle so we could commence the hard work ahead with a cool and steady hand. A writing metaphor served me well here: "One must be fresh when facing the blank page, *n'est-ce pas*? Otherwise, we invite catastrophe."

"How would *you* know?" F. said, smirking. "You're not *really* a writer—remember?"

"*Touché*," I said, laughing. "I almost forgot."

He laughed too. I "threw on some clothes," as the Americans say, and we glided over to the corner drugstore, Schwab's— our weariness overruled by the revivifying effect of purposeful expectancy and patriotic zeal. It was barely light out. The meek early sunlight was like a comforting thin blanket. Hungry hummingbirds were already up and at 'em, searching for nectar, purring with their beautiful little violence of motion. The night-blooming jasmine and gardenias were redolent as ever, testifying to the sweet sanctity of those who, dauntless, pursue the inextinguishable torch of truth.

Yes, Hy, it felt wonderful to be alive again, and to know the mission is worth fighting for—a feeling that was only enhanced once we entered the drugstore.

It was half past Six. They had just opened and there was a new girl behind the counter, being shown the ropes by an older waitress. She had inherited someone else's uniform (the embroidered name in the upper left corner didn't match the one she was called), and it was too small—showing nearly everything she had to show, in just the right places. I suggested sitting at the counter, but Fitzgerald had already turned toward the tables. I'm such an animal, really. Desire nearly always overwhelms me when my defenses are down—when I'm tired, happy, or sad. All the time, I guess. I do believe I'm a gentleman as far as the general welfare of humanity is concerned; but when it comes to women, I'm a beast, I fear. I'd sooner copulate with a fine-looking lady than talk to her and pass the time of day.

Anyway, the waitress in training was far too busy to accommodate what I had in mind. The pungent aroma of grilled bacon supplanted one lust with another. Mr. Fitzgerald and I ate a huge breakfast of hotcakes, ham, eggs, bacon, and juice. We shared it like two gluttons, laughing gutturally, even as the agents, writers, directors, and producers (apparently it was too early for actors and actresses) began to dribble in. Mr. Fitzgerald eyed them all with contempt—especially once we were done and he had nothing but his coffee and cigarettes to distract him.

"Look at them," he said dreamily, while looking at nothing himself. "They know nothing. Each is dependent upon what the others think. None of them trusts his own opinion, not even for a second."

"Oh, they're not that bad, are they? Just a bunch of storytellers."

"With no vision."

"They have eyes."

"On the surface—but I see underneath."

"So, you're better than everybody else?"

"Is that so strange? Somebody must be the best. Obviously, you thought so; otherwise, you wouldn't be going to all this trouble, would you?"

"Nobody's the best, and nobody's the worst. There's always somebody better or worse than you are—everybody's got a different opinion."

"Yes, yes, I know."

"You were testing me, weren't you?"

"Perhaps—though I do strive for greatness. It takes a certain greatness to even make the attempt—wouldn't you say?"

Mr. Fitzgerald's a nice guy, I've decided, when he isn't trying to convince everyone—including himself, foremost—that he's an immortal talent. Isn't it enough to try to be good and to do good work without constantly telling everybody about it and worrying aloud about whether you're going to be remembered by people you don't even know? I'd rather share a few good times and laughs right now than revel in the intangible fantasy that a slew of strangers might appreciate that I could turn a nice phrase. Fitzgerald isn't the only writer with this affliction, of course. I've known a few in my day (excluding you, of course, Hy—journalists don't count, at least not negatively). What nuts. But I can't let it get to me.

I got the check, fast. Mr. Fitzgerald stayed behind to read *Variety*—it helped him procrastinate, so he wouldn't have to go home to adapt his short story for Shirley Temple. Outside, the fresh daily papers were stacked up in rows. Refusing to be burdened by more of what I already knew, I averted my eyes from their depressing headlines.

I am at peace for the moment and will catch a few hours sleep now, Hyman. And though I toss and turn, that's only because I'm suddenly filled with unbridled optimism. Yes, my dearest friend, my heart is full of joy and hope for France.

Your friend,
Henri

Dear Hy,

Fitzgerald is driving me crazy! We may be getting more than we bargained for with him. Physically, the man's a terrible hypochondriac and a lazy sow bug to boot, but his mind is never at rest—which may sound impressive, but it's not. He's like an overloaded circuit setting off sparks and causing static. His crazy scheming drives me crazy. It's everything I can do to get him to keep a secret.

First, he shows me a letter he's written to Franklin Roosevelt, asking for assistance in our cause. I tore it up immediately! Then he begs me to allow Zelda to become involved, thinking the change, however drastic, would do her good ("She needs to believe she's doing something important," he's whined to me repeatedly). He's so sure it would save her. The poor woman has just been released from a mental hospital, and she's living with her mother in Montgomery, Alabama. I'm not doubting Fitzgerald completely, but even if she were a Mata Hari for the Allies, we'd have no use for her. He says he agrees with me—and then a few hours later he calls me at the hotel and starts in on the same thing all over again.

Don't fret, though. I don't think he's said anything to her.

I've threatened to cancel the mission if he does—and I have his acknowledgment in writing. Don't laugh! Fitzgerald started it. Yesterday evening, he showed up at the hotel with a typed document. I have a copy of it before me now. I won't bore you with its painfully banal pseudo-legal prose. The point is that he insists on securing full publishing rights to any factual or fictional material arising from our projected exploits. This is extremely important to him. Apparently, his wife has borrowed from their mutual experiences for her own writing, and this has been an anathema to Mr. Fitzgerald's creative integrity—or so he says. I assured him that I would have no interest in writing about him or our adventures for the purposes of publication. After all, I am not a professional writer. Whatever latent literary interest I may have possessed is rapidly evaporating into thin air the more I get to know Mr. Fitzgerald.

I shouldn't take him so seriously—and I won't, whenever I can help it. But he was so damn insistent I sign his stupid agreement (I did, of course), it just made me mad. So, I made up my own agreement:

> *I, F. Scott Fitzgerald, do solemnly swear that I shall keep all conversations, interactions, and discussions involving myself and Henri Duval strictly confidential. From this day forward, I shall never speak or write of any matter regarding my acquaintance with Mr. Duval without Mr. Duval's express permission ("Unless Duval dies or the present war in Europe is terminated." F.S. F.).*

Hilarious, isn't it? And now I shall tear it up. . . . There. Nothing on paper matters a jot, after all, unless a man's word is good. That is what I'm counting on.

Here is something on paper that does matter, our initial correspondence designed to open a critical and essential door for
our cause:

Dear Marshal Pétain,

I trust all is well with you. Through various channels, I have
heard that the recent mood is one of cautious optimism, and I
must say I have been feeling the same way. If we can convince
Hitler and his ilk that our intentions are conciliatory, then we
are sure to succeed in securing stable enough relations with
them to heal our wounds—and perhaps, in time, they will see
that our interests are not as dissimilar as we had once thought.
A strong France can assure a strong Germany, and vice versa.
After all, it is a stalemate, as you've said. Neither the Allies
nor Hitler can win in the long run, and we'll end up destroying
each other unless we *both* agree to make concessions to ensure
a lasting peace. This is a sensible definition of collaboration,
as I understand it.

I have been able to make some contact with the Nazi
underground here, and they seem sympathetic and appreciative of my efforts to further a more humane perspective on the
Nazi intent. My alias is working well, though it does feel a wee
bit absurd and embarrassing (as I know we have discussed)
to be sneaking about when there is nothing to hide. As soon
as the anti-Nazi sentiment abates a bit more, then perhaps I
shall be allowed to give up this charade of being a writer. For
now, I realize it's best to pull the strings behind the scenes, for
the Americans—being the Anglophiles they are at heart— do

detest the Axis powers. One cannot blame them entirely, as far as Hitler is concerned. But that is another subject—and of course it is not entirely impossible that, flushed with victory as he surely is now, the ecstasies of triumphant achievement will tame him somewhat and temper what some have termed his "megalomania."

Success makes many men kind, and we shall see with Hitler. As you know, if he is to realize his will to power, the commander-in-chief must be hard as stone, merciless, and predatory, too. Yes, every man must spur himself onward to scale untold heights. Any suffering he endures is self-induced, ultimately, and the flagellant lashes himself into deification by eliminating all fallible or impure purposes, and thus controlling his own destiny. There is good to be had in this alliance if only we can reach a mutual understanding of each other's outstanding qualities.

But I do go on. Please indulge me. After all, I haven't spoken to an architect for months, and I've immersed myself in this world of cinema artists. One is a famous author—interestingly, he is a fervent admirer of yours. His name is F. Scott Fitzgerald. I somehow recall you having mentioned that you were fond of a few of the American expatriate novelists. He knows nothing of my official capacity, but he has been in abject awe of me ever since I told him that I am acquainted with you. He has said that he wishes he could tell you what a splendid job he thinks you're doing. "Under any circumstances, France could not be in better hands"—these were his very words, I think. Like all of us, he'd like to get his hands around that traitor de Gaulle's neck.

I am sure this is foolishly untimely, but he is one of those people who is forever cultivating the acquaintance of the famous—not that I blame him, especially considering his own formidable reputation in the book world. He has begged me to be allowed to send you his felicitations in his own words.

Please ignore this request! I convey it merely because I thought you might be interested to know that the true artists and intellectuals of this rather benighted country truly do appreciate you for what you are, dear grand marshal. And if Mr. Fitzgerald is representative of an exemplary intellectual trend about the new France, then perhaps we might investigate the possibility of employing him in some visible capacity as a spokesman. I'm not exactly sure how to proceed with this (or if you even wish me to consider doing so), but it is a thought.

My very best to everyone, especially Laval.

Yours truly,
Henri Duval

PS: I had a dream—a sort of blueprint vision, really—for that new addition to the Ermitage.[4] Here is a little sketch:

4. Pétain's small farm on the Riviera in Villeneuve-Loubet, between Nice and Antibes, and near Vence—where the marshal returned to the soil on occasional weekends, especially during the annual September grape harvest in his five-acre vineyard. (ed.)

I would love to talk to you about it. Until then, my very best wishes.

Well, Hy, now that you've probably finished throwing up over that twisted travesty of thought, I know you'll forgive me as you know as well that it is all subterfuge. I have had some regrets, though, as to its effectiveness: Did I try too hard? Did I go on too much about Hitler? Oh, well, it's too late. I've sent it already.

July 17, 1940

Hyman,

I don't know how much more of this I can stand!

The last two weeks have been an eternity, I'm telling you. First, my job came through at Paramount. That's where I'm writing you from (you may have noticed the letterhead). I suppose I should be amused with my present situation. I have been here eight days, and they have yet to tell me what to do. I call my immediate superior—head "story editor" is his title, I believe— every morning upon arriving at my tiny office. He thanks me for phoning him and tells me to check back with him tomorrow if I haven't heard from him later today. They're saving me for projects with a foreign flavor, he says, because most of their writers can't "cut the mustard on making the European stuff wash." I have no idea what this means, but I'm sure it's what he said because he's used the same phrase three or four times now. I'm always afraid I'll expose my ignorance by asking him to explain. If this is "lingo," as they say, it hasn't appeared in any of the scenario writing manuals I've studied. I must make a note of this, so I won't keep forgetting to ask Mr. Fitzgerald about it.

There is a lot of fast talk here. You should see these Hollywood theatrical agents. At least a half dozen who specialize in literary representation have either called or marched right into my office in just the few short days I've been here. They're like buzzards circling a fresh carcass. Some of them chomp cigars as they talk; some look like they're just out of diapers. At first, I was very self-conscious with them. I thought they would expect to discuss literature and the current state of the cinema. I prattled on at length, comparing Eisenstein to Dostoyevsky, Tolstoy to D.W. Griffith, and then, tongue-in-cheek, *Moby Dick* to *The Scarlet Letter*—considering how they relate to the somewhat lecherous quest for the successful commercial film. And all I got were blank stares or circumlocution, demonstrating that they know even less about the literary enterprise than I do. I don't think they have ever read a book or seen a movie that they can remember, let alone discuss in the most rudimentary intellectual way. How odd and how appalling that they are so presumptuous as to urge you to let them pilot your career (for a price—ten percent of all your earnings). "Where?" I might ask if I weren't so desperately intent on blending in with the background.

It's nerve-wracking, of course. But work, if you can call it that, is the least of my problems. I give the agents a sincere nod and tell them I'll think about their propositions, and they go away. But Fitzgerald does not. I wouldn't mind if he weren't such a hypochondriacal, neurotic, egotistical pansy! It's gotten so bad that I've taken to calling him by his Christian name, Frances. Boy, does he ever hate it when you call him Frances. It's the only thing that will make him see red long enough to push himself during our daily exercise regimen. The man is so shiftless and lackadaisical, and downright cowardly in physical matters, that he is literally afraid to sweat. He has many reasons for this, but I think I'd lose my mind if I tried to recall them for you. For the purpose of the mission I am doing what I can to beat his shamelessly neglected physique into something resembling the standard human body as it was meant to be—not the grotesque, gin-bloated, shaved man-sloth that he is. Suffice it to say that seeing the man in a bathing suit for the first time gave me such a queasy feeling that I recall being grateful I had not yet had breakfast.

Of course, if this stale, undefined fleshy dough wasn't my charge and first responsibility, it really wouldn't bother me. I'd shrug my shoulders and forget it. But this is what I must work with. Our daily schedule for the next three to six weeks is as follows (I pray we'll have this much time, although the war will not simply adjourn itself to allow us optimum conditions for our preparation):

Monday ~ running, light sparring (Santa Monica Beach)
Ocean swim (S. M. Beach)

Tuesday ~ bicycling (Hollywood—Muscle Beach)
Weightlifting, jump rope, cycle home

Wednesday ~ running, light sparring, swim (S.M. Beach)

Thursday ~ cycling, weights, jump rope

Friday ~ Run, spar, swim

Saturday ~ Run or swim (Santa Monica Beach)

Sunday ~ Run or swim (optional)

It sounds much more rigorous than it is. Running, to Frances, is staggering a few yards one way, then stopping for a cigarette, crawling back to the starting line, plopping down on his beach towel, and refusing to move until he drinks a Coca-Cola. After we spar (with gloves so heavy and cumbersome, you couldn't knock out a fly with them), he insists on rewarding himself with a candy bar. Then, after the swim, we stop at a small diner on the boardwalk so he can have some hot cocoa to take away his chill. I feel as if I'm training a tired old beast for his last chance to join the circus. Our antics abroad are unlikely to be physically grueling, I might add, but you never know. One must always be prepared. And we must be swift in our escape.

You will notice that except for Saturday and Sunday, I alternate between cycling and running, for the legs; sparring and jumping rope, for quickness and agility (and self-defense, of course). The swimming is for endurance and as a restorative for the muscle strain of the weights and all the other activities. We do everything by the sea, except the cycling: running on the apron of the shore; jumping rope on the boardwalk by the pier; sparring on sand, boardwalk, or at the end of the pier; lifting weights at a public facility on the sand. On running days, Mr. Fitzgerald and I take separate cars. I arrive forty minutes early (5:20 a.m.) so I can take my morning exercise (I run 10 kilometers) before supervising Fitzgerald at his elephantine pace (he has yet to run two consecutive kilometers, even as I pace him like a peasant walking a donkey). The cycling is not as bad as it would seem. Fitzgerald is, after all, stronger than he thinks, and I think he enjoys riding his bicycle more than anything else. He also does a great deal of coasting; in addition, on the long hills, he'll contrive some excuse to check his tire pressure, inevitably, or spot some phenomenon of nature that so astounds him he must point excitedly and pause (blue jays, an heiress, a wolf—though I've yet to bear witness to these convenient fancies). As far as the sparring, fisticuffs is his strong suit, though unfortunately he's abysmally lazy (and deluded—a byproduct of his sloth). He's the sort of fellow who spends more time admiring some little achievement than breaking the hard ground and doing the real work. He'll rock me with an unexpected punch, then lower his hands and stand back to grin smugly, instead of following up immediately with more (and harder) firepower. Also, in resigning himself to his deteriorated condition, he has developed an insane conviction that form and style can compensate for substance. I've nearly stunned him with my retaliatory frustration several times already—and I've explained the basis of my anger—but the man won't listen to me. He smiles cagily, tells me what I'm really talking about is his writing, then he goes into the water without waiting for me (we swim a few hundred yards—I intend to build him up to a kilometer, at least).

My only consolation is the time I spend alone before Mr. Fitzgerald arrives at six, on the running days. The air is so crisp and fresh in the California early mornings, you feel as if you're being born with the day. The quiet gives you a certain freedom, as if the world is yours. You share a sweet secret with the milkman, the paperboy, and other early risers—they're all in your employ. Everything is alive and just waiting for you to nod and say yes. You accept everything because you aren't awake yet. If anything displeases you there's not enough of it to offend you. What's good persists in visionary splendor; what's corrupt or unseemly goes away with nothing more than a wince. This is what it's like to fall in love with a beautiful foreign place . . . or woman . . .

Yes, there is another woman, alas. She's there at the apron of the sea or in the water every morning as I trot by, my lungs heaving happily. She is a dream. I'm not even certain I want her

"SHE'S THERE AT THE APRON OF THE SEA OR IN THE WATER EVERY MORNING AS I TROT BY..."

to be real. It's not that I don't want to seduce her. I do, most definitely—but I want her so violently that I feel weak-kneed about it. I look at this lithe, lone Venus, and she reminds me of no one. I've never fallen for a woman who reminds me of no one. In the past, this sense of the familiar facilitates the desired conquest, but also trivializes it, so that even as I make love to a stranger I feel as if I've touched her and talked to her before. I've *had* her already. She is nothing new to me.

But this one is. I don't know what it is about her. I adore her, though I've never exchanged a word with her, and I'm not even sure she's taken notice of me. A bizarre impulse—romantic love. I'm sure I'll get over it. What do I need with another dumb American blonde?

Today's post was just delivered. It is self-explanatory. We have now received a response to my letter—from the source:

Dear Henri,

Thank you for reporting on the climate in Hollywood. It is a good thing that you have struck up an acquaintance with the famous writer Fitzgerald, but please don't prattle on as you do about our new friend Adolph. This is a situation with which we must contend. There is nothing else to say about it.

Yes, I would be glad to hear from Mister Fitzgerald. I think I have read some of his things. *Tender Is the Farewell to Morning*—isn't that his? Oh, yes—something about paradise, too. I liked that very much. I loved the American songs from that story—such good music—it's still my favorite. But who has time for dancing these days? It's a shame, isn't it? If the Germans knew how to have a civilized good time, I doubt they'd be such a problem to everybody.

I've never written anything made-up, I'm sure you know. But I've been thinking about a story for many years— about a general who marries a lovely woman who it turns out is of ill-repute. There is a threat of scandal, and the general must have this woman removed, violently. But his love for this lady prevents him from having his orders executed in her regard. He manages to quell the rumors about her, and she proves herself an extraordinary wife (in every sense!). But then her past rears its foul insidious head in the form of the terrible disease she harbors as an emblem of her sin. He dies a painful, slow death.

This story has haunted me. I would write it except people would think it is true! Perhaps if I take a pen name and set the events during the time of the French Revolution. There are so many different things one may do with a story. It is somewhat like a battle, in that regard. One struggles for the proper strategy, keeping in mind the old approaches, then using them up to accommodate whatever new advances are considered, then approved—then into combat, with victory certain if the ingenuity and dedication are sound.

It would be so simple to be a writer if one applied the right angle of attack to it.

Yours sincerely,
Phillipe [Pétain—*Ed.*]

[Henri Duval's reaction letter to Marshal Pétain's undated letter has neither date nor heading, but clearly follows in sequence at this point in the clandestine correspondence. *Ed.*]

That's it, Hy. We can't say, at this point, whether that slippery old sardine is hooked, but we've got him interested, don't you think? I spent much of last night and this morning working with Mr. Fitzgerald on his reply (we cancelled our exercise today). First, he was a bit disappointed. He had expected a gushing fan letter filled with unreserved, informed admiration—not the doddering, slightly incoherent ramblings of a sick demented old man. That Pétain confused one of his titles with Hemingway's was unpardonable—he was so furious at first that I couldn't talk to him. Pétain was an "ignoramus" and "dilettante" who knew nothing about literature. When I agreed, he was somewhat appeased.

Not that it matters much. I don't know if it can be attributed to his agitation over the marshal's letter, but I have never seen a human being make more of a shambles out of committing words to paper. His contention was that the careful, dedicated writer must refine his choices by saying what he has to say in as many ways as he can, and then choosing the most effective. At the rate he was going it would have taken the man six months to write his first letter; needless to say, I had to take over. I've placated him by complimenting him on his one little sentence (culled from Verlaine), labored over for endless hours: "Dear Marshal Pétain: It rains in my heart as it rains on the town: My innermost soul bursts with sorrowful pride, as you have granted my most cherished request to correspond with such a time-honored and revered, historic person. Thank you, sir . . ."

I don't know why he must be so breathless about the written word. For the most part, he speaks plainly. I don't know why he can't write a lucid, monochromatic sentence if he can speak one. Regardless, I've urged him not to corrupt his craft by rushing himself—a good excuse which allows me to take over—and

he doesn't seem to mind. So, I have taken the helm. He did fill
in little details. He also lectured me on the importance of punc-
tuation consistency. That was one hour down the drain until I
distracted him by being distracted myself—by thoughts of that
lovely blonde siren from the beach at Santa Monica.

"What are you thinking about?" he asked.

"A woman I hope to meet," I said.

"Romance is a glandular problem," he joked, trying to be
cynical. The jocular tone tapered off, losing resonance. He lit a
cigarette to patch the fissure in his proffered amorality.

Am I becoming like Fitzgerald? I see that lovely angel's face,
with just the vaguest trace of pinchable pudginess that follows
proportionately with her ripened bust and thighs (her ankles
and arms are exceedingly well-turned, delicate to a fault, by
comparison), then the slightest touch of dovelike pallor in the
downturned slope of her neck when entering or leaving the
water—and I want to offer myself to her on my knees. I have
this terrible desire to pour my soul out to this uncharted territo-
ry, and I feel so utterly void in my own psychical vortex—alien
to myself (as I never am!) until I imagine her unburdening herself with me.

And then I stop spinning. My fantasies anchor onto my
obsessive dream of the two of us. When she removes her bathing cap and shakes her hair out, it catches the fresh morning
light like golden honey dripping into my eyes and mouth. I can
taste such a sight. She ignores me, yes, but she does continue
to come here at the same time every day. She's waiting for my
approach, I think—why am I suddenly so shy? I'm a little out
of practice, I'll admit, as far as my ordinary philandering habits
back home, but this fragile woman terrifies me. I can't talk to
her, though I know I must.

Here is the end result of the tortuous creative labors between Mr. Fitzgerald and myself to come up with an effective responsive plea to the target which will further this critical acquaintance:

Dear Marshal Pétain,

It rains in my heart as it rains on the town: My innermost soul bursts with sorrowful pride as you have granted my most cherished request—to correspond with such a time-honored and revered, historic person. Thank you, sir. Though I am as American as our fair land's red, white, and blue, I adore France and all things French—as you must know from my writing. I met many of my dearest friends in your country, and when I think of my happy times with them at wonderful places like le Dome, la Coupole, le Select, Ciros, the Cap d'Antibes, Juan-les-Pins, and the Place de la Groupe, I would weep with sheer delight at such treasured memories were it not for the uncertainty I now feel at the prospect of being able to return to see the Paris and the Riviera I knew and loved —in an atmosphere of joyous festivity and celebration, permeated by the so subtle ambient illumination of joie de vivre that the Impressionists understood so well—for *light* itself, in every aspect of its refractory aesthetics, seminally derives from the very essence of France's spirit.

If anyone can make those happy tears (and the tears of everyone else I know) flow once again, it is you. You have my fullest confidence and pride. As all true Americans and earnest citizens of the world are thankful to see, France is safe with you, Marshal Pétain. I shan't keep you from the more urgent matters of your calling, except to thank you once again for bestowing this sacred privilege upon yet another of your lowly admirers. I wouldn't dare to presume in your case, but if I may be of any assistance to you in any capacity whatsoever as you chart the sure course of your ingenious contribution to modern (and classic) literature, please feel free to demand of me whatever you will. In a general substantive sense, my editorial instincts are adept; I've served as a willing sounding board for many of the finest talents of our time. Although, in this instance, regarding your formidable talents, I realize I'm overstepping my bounds. For you are already France's most notable historian—as evidenced, of course, by what you have already done (despicable de Gaulle was shameless, I know, weaseling in on the authorship). Even so, I would give anything to assist in whatever small way I can, if you have any use for my humble talents.

Last but not least, I would be indebted to you beyond the bounds of my own life—and all of America would be grateful—if, in the great generosity of your heart, you would allow me to visit you (at your convenience, but soon) so that America might hear your thoughts on the important world issues. I am friendly with editors at most of the major magazines, and I know they would give their eye teeth for this rare privilege. But I wouldn't dare proceed a centimeter without first possessing your encouragement and approval.

Patiently awaiting your rightful decision regarding these matters, I shall forever remain

Your faithful American servant,
F. Scott Fitzgerald

PARAMOUNT STUDIOS

West Coast Studios

HOLLYWOOD, CALIF.

Telephone: Hollywood-2422 // Cable: FamFilm

July 18, 1940

Hyman,

By nature, I had thought I would always be a philanderer. Maybe I still am—after all, this is all very new. But I have never encountered such a giddy, cliffhanging, heart-in-the-throat feeling. Is this how you felt upon falling in love with Gertrude? I hope not. Frankly, I am not sure that I enjoy being in such a state. I've always been ruled by my passions, but this is something else. "If you have an itch, scratch it," I think my motto has been. But this is like breaking out in hives—it monopolizes you. You want to rip your head off to keep from thinking about it. And the only remedy is the irritant itself—her. Nothing else will do.

The day began simply enough. I drove to the beach at my usual time. The early morning was no more miraculous than normal—no fog, just the crisp blue sky starched at its edges by the usual fringe of decorative cumulus. All very containable and finite—until I began my little trot and spied her frolicking shoreward on the crest of a small breaker. She bounced over a short fall into the wave's trough and glided forward wreathed by a passionate froth of brilliant whitewater, her arms hugging her sides to create a streamlining effect which allowed her to expropriate surprising reserves of propulsive strength from the otherwise docile looking sea.

Having all but drifted from view, the wispy clouds had suddenly pulled back the curtain on a celestial void. Sea and sky swirled together, engulfing whatever remained of me.

Dizzily, I rushed toward her. I poured perspiration, feeling utterly clammy and faint—me, a near-Olympic athlete who, sixteen years ago, might have brought France a medal in long distance if I had not been ill during the qualifications. Even with a high fever, I was not so weakened then as now, after just a few minutes of exertion. She had floated into shore, and she stood, facing me in the shallows, smiling just a little. I could not wave or extend even the shortest greeting; in the next moment, she was going to remove her cap. Fearful that the sheer beauty of that casual act would drop me to my knees, I looked askance and slammed into something small and soft. It screeched maniacally—and then so did I. A little brown dog—a dachshund, I saw now—had bitten my toe.

The dog was all right. I was the one who was injured. It circled me and yelped ferociously. I stopped running, to avoid stepping on it again, and saw that my toe was bleeding.

"No, no, ne-no! B-bad dog—bad!"

I jerked about. She was standing before me. Her flesh-colored bathing cap hadn't been removed, since this rude incident of which I was reluctant star had intervened. "I am so s-sorry," she said with sweet contriteness, betraying what I now realized was a slight speech pathology that I immediately adored with-

out pity or surprise, but rather a sense of mad necessity, as if everything about her—the few laugh wrinkles about the eyes, the slight gravidness in the hips—every imperfection was so perfect that together they anchored my focus of the natural art of her.

I was speechless.

"You've had a shock," she said. "Sit d-down."

The tide lapped over my feet.

"Good. L-let the w-water cleanse your t-toe . . ."

"You are so very kind," I managed, by habit thickening my accent; being in the throes of abject desperation, I could only trust to my basest, most accessible and familiar instincts.

"K-kind, n-nothing. My dog b-bit you."

The creature in question, being a slave to his protective instincts, had renewed his threat as his dear master approached me. She splashed him, and he moved off a foot or two, yelped a bit, and settled down.

She removed her cap and returned my stunned, vacant stare with the sweetest, most grateful little smile. It shamed me into willing servitude; my only compensation was that it loosened my tongue. I was no longer afraid to converse. Now, I felt compelled to do so.

"I want to know everything about you," I said before I could censor myself and proceed at a more moderate pace.

To my relief, she was not taken aback.

"I see you every morning," she said, nodding, confirming our previous acquaintance.

"I am so grateful your dog bit me."

We laughed together—beginning nervously but ending in a chorus of cheery expectation.

"You m-must be shy," she ventured.

"Ordinarily, I am not," I told her. "What about you?"

She was so shy about herself, I can't tell you. I feel as if I have known her forever, and yet even after having spoken with her for more than an hour, I can hardly tell you more than her Christian name: Heather. She has a marvelous sense of humor. It takes her quite a while to get things out sometimes, but that only makes the rejoinder or punch line more effective or amusing. She's from Ohio, visiting an aunt and trying to make up her mind whether she wants to move here. She has been married and divorced and refuses to discuss any part of it other than to say she has made up her mind to not regret anything. She seems so worldly for a schoolteacher. I was surprised. And she's very sad about France, she says. She wishes she could do something about those Germans and desperately wants to visit Paris someday.

"I would love to take you, if I could."

Our easy-going conversation came to a halt. We looked deeply into each other's eyes.

"That would be w-wonderful," she said.

She became tearful suddenly and turned away. She stood up now, and so did I. Her little dachshund came running to her. Thankfully she shooed it away.

I stepped toward her. "Don't be sad," I urged her. "France will be free again. You'll see. Our spirit is stronger than you think."

"It's not that . . . Why are you being so nice?"

"I am very attracted to you."

She turned around. "W-would you like to m-make love to me?"

We rushed into each other's arms. I couldn't describe the feeling—or the kiss.

"I do not want to take advantage of you," I said, once I got my breath back. "I *have* taken advantage of the other women in my life, but you are different."

She told me she was just a woman.

I told her I was just a man.

She took my hand and led me into that celestial sea. Everything was spinning, dizzy, soaring. I was faint with desire as she locked her limbs about my waist. We were face to face, swimming in each other's eyes.

"I'm a terrible philanderer."

"You're m-married?"

"No."

"Then what's the problem?"

"I have a keen sense, like your little hound—for women in trouble. You're trying to forget someone or hurt somebody who has hurt you. I knew when I first saw you."

She wept in my arms. Reflexively, her thighs tightened about my waist. "I l-like it that you w-want me. Isn't that enough?"

"Any man in his right mind would fall in love with you."

"G-good." She squirmed out of her bathing suit and wrapped it around her arm, tying it on like a tourniquet, for safekeeping.

"P-please . . . I n-need you to take advantage of m-me."

"No. No. I can't. We shouldn't."

"I was g-going to drown myself—I've b-been trying to."

I could not believe what she was saying: a creature of such exquisite and unique beauty on the verge of extinction? "Oh no."

"Y-yes. I l-like you. We f-found each other. It's not b-bad. It's g-good . . . and I'm g-getting cold!"

"M-me, too," I stammered, surprisingly.

We laughed in harmony as we blended with the sea and sky!

July 21, 1940

Dear Hyman,

Love has made me a different man—thank God, as presently I need all the strength of character I can muster to withstand the nerve-wracking frustrations of my association with Frances (as I've been calling that poor excuse for a man). It's not so much that the miserable wretch questions my authority. Instead, he has an air of irredeemable, unmitigated lassitude that incenses me to no end. It explains, at least in part, his preposterous physical decrepitude.

My view of Fitzgerald has changed dramatically, and fast. I should have anticipated much of this daily uphill struggle, but I was so focused on trying to set up the end game I didn't think about it. You've got to wonder what caused him to become this way. I think it's a peculiarly American trait: an abhorrence for hard labor, be it mental or physical. I would bet my last franc that the slang term "short cut" derives from Americanese. Americans know that work is necessary but don't want to do it. They want to find a way around it or fool someone else into doing it for them. Like pouting children, they seem to be in passive rebellion against their indentured puritan ancestry. Hence, we fight on in darkness against the goddamn Nazis, with America's full "moral" support.

Ha!

Well, Frances doesn't see why the running and rigorous exercise is necessary. He's become positively mutinous in this regard. I've gone to great lengths, as I'm sure I've told you, to indicate that I'm not doing this for my own amusement—that the goal here is two-fold, to prepare him mentally and phys-ically, so that he will accomplish what he's been recruited to do, while being in the very best state of preparedness possi-ble, under the circumstances, to have at least some chance of surviving the ordeal as he and I attempt our escape. For God's sake—as it stands now, the man can hardly climb a flight of stairs without getting out of breath. We have made some prog-ress, yes, but it's this lethargic attitude, as I said, that is our biggest obstacle by far.

"You're a glutton for punishment," he's forever telling me. This remark is the smuggest of threats, a tell-tale sign that he's about to let himself wind down. He'll stop suddenly—like a stubborn mule—and refuse to go on. I have seen him swing off his bicycle and pause with it in the middle of traffic!

"But life *is* punishment!" I scream back at him, the veins bursting in my neck. This is what the rigorous strain of exer-cise teaches. Yes, exercise is hard. Life is hard—even when it seems easy. The easier things are, the more we forget the pain in store for us. The coup de grâce is always the punch the fight-er doesn't see! The pain of rigorous physical exertion reminds us we must be circumspect—we must gird our loins so that we can contend with life's disasters and not be destroyed by them.

Doesn't this make sense to you, Hy? It's clear enough, I think, but Mr. Fitzgerald is forever arguing with me. The only thing that keeps him in line is my threat to call the whole thing off.

I'm smoking heavily again, and I seem to have acquired a taste for American whiskey (never in Fitzgerald's presence). Not that I can't help it, but the man just makes me nervous. I worry that his indulgent lassitude is going to get us both killed once we launch our somewhat overambitious plan. If he'd only apply himself to the cause as he applies himself to his infernal stories—the significance of which pales in comparison with the more pressing matters at hand. Who cares about the exploits of a washed-up hack scenario writer named Pat Hobby when civilization, as we know it, is crumbling!

Not fair, no. Mr. Fitzgerald does care passionately about his fictional creations, I believe, and he also cares about the war. Art and politics. Perhaps if there were more of the former, there would be less of the latter. Quite true, really. Then, what is my problem? Fitzgerald, his high-strung disposition, the strain of keeping him in line, my job at the studio (I live in constant fear of being called upon to write) . . . and now, Heather too.

She's even lovelier than I expected or hoped. She has done nothing but dazzle me with her sparkling charms. There is such warmth to this woman, my face hurts from smiling. I'm hoarse from our incessant chattering and laughter. I find myself spilling both seed and soul to this captivating creature. It must be somewhat akin to how a woman feels as she is ready to deliver her young—that pushing feeling. I want to give all of myself to life, which is this woman. I have had to reign in my innermost thoughts with her—though instinctively I desperately desire to share my every thought and feeling, as I am sure she has with me.

This is my only difficulty—that I must conceal so much

from her. She knows how I feel about her, but I will not say the word *love*. It will only make parting such awful sorrow for us. Being unable to tell her what I am really doing here in America gnaws at me. I will not tell her, for fear of getting her involved. But it hurts me to be deceitful—and angers me, too, I must admit. Deceit, however innocent or well-intended, can fester and spread. I want nothing to be tainted between us. But duty dictates that I must make do under the circumstances.

Hopefully, I will be able to share this all with her someday. Luckily, this tug of war inside me doesn't seem to be the least bit apparent to her. I blush to tell you how wonderful she thinks I am. I know I'm your ordinary run-of-the-mill scamp and scoundrel, but love is so blissfully blind, you know. We're entitled to fall prey to it as our little hearts desire. It is every human being's inalienable right to be as demented with love as he or she likes. I certainly am.

Yes, so giddy with delight, but so guilt-stricken, too, which accounts for the clammy palpitations (and, regretfully, the mawkish tone of this letter—I'm sorry, but communicating with you is so invaluable in helping me think things through, incalculably so!). She thinks we are beginning something enduring, and what I cannot tell her (and can hardly accept) is that it is much more likely that in two months' time I shall be dead.

Your friend,
Henri

Hollywood, California
July 23, 1940

Hyman,

I can't tell you how ill I am from aggravation—but I will try, as I have all the time in the world today.

I called in sick to Paramount and have been lolling about the pool at the hotel. A half hour ago, that albino-haired lizard, Ava Baker, showed up to slither around the patio for the afternoon. She must have half the staff here in her partial employ (you can imagine how she must pay her bills!), as I'm certain she's neither guest nor resident of the Garden, and they make a very stern practice of barring all freeloaders and riffraff from the grounds. She is given access to the premises because she is a ready and willing actress looking for work the easy way. Perhaps I'm jealous because she snubbed me by asking Fritz Brunheimer, the well-known émigré director, to rub the cocoa butter on her back. I feel cheap and used—though I did get what I deserved, however petty and short-sighted that is. But I also feel relieved, for if she had insisted on carrying on with me, it would have been too much for me to bear now. I have my hands full beyond my wildest dreams with *Marion*.

That's right. You see, Marion is Heather—or I should say Heather is really Marion.

Let me explain. Just this morning, we met as usual at the beach. I brought a thermos of coffee and some bread and jam. The fog was thick and cold, so we sought refuge in my Ford, and camped out there, eating and chatting and whatnot, and time flew quite furiously on its silent wings. As we were saying goodbye, Mr. Fitzgerald appeared. He startled us, as I think had been his intent.

"What d'ya say?"

Our embrace severed of itself. We stood apart, straightening our skimpy beach clothes.

"Sir, you're early."

"Late," he said, smiling slyly.

"Oh."

"Hello," my lady was saying, as if prompting me to step on it with the introductions.

"I'm so sorry. Scott Fitzgerald, Heather Williams. Heather, this is my friend, Scott."

Fitzgerald looked at both of us as if we were in on a joke he expected us to share.

Momentarily, "Heather" began smiling in that same roguish way. She fussed with herself a bit, cinching the belt of her striped cotton twill beach dress, smoothing her lovely hair with rather nervous fingers, then searching for the overlarge smoked glasses in her bag and putting them on. "You l-look familiar," she told Fitzgerald, nodding.

"*Heather?*" Fitzgerald asked, his voice rising comically high. "Hi ya, *Heather.*" He bent over laughing, planting hands on both knees.

"What is so funny?" I demanded.

He straightened and came close to my love. "Do you know who *I* am, *Heather?*"

"N-no."

"Well, I'm Ernest Hemingway, the famous bullslinger."

"N-no."

"Don't you remember me?" he asked, suddenly doleful.

She was decidedly uncomfortable, at the disadvantage in Mr. Fitzgerald's little game.

"Scott *Fitzgerald*, the author—*Marion*. You didn't recognize me without my better half."

"Scott, Scott, it's b-been years. H-how are you?"

"Fine, Marion. Just fine."

"Would someone care to explain this to me?" I interjected.

She rushed to my side, burying herself in my sweater. "I w-was going to tell you, b-but first I wanted us to have fun together and it might not have h-happened otherwise."

Ever the gentleman, Mr. Fitzgerald finally inquired as to whether he was intruding at an indelicate moment.

I looked to Marion for answer and explanation. She responded by saying, "F-follow me."

She ran out onto the sand and proceeded north along the shore, looking back over her shoulder and beckoning us to follow. We proceeded at a quick clip.

Fitzgerald laughed. "Don't you know who she is?"

"You must tell me," I demanded.

"It's *her* surprise," he said happily, his cheeks blooming with the thrill of being party to the romantic intrigue of which I was victim. It gave him the upper hand, and he liked it.

As we walked, I couldn't get a thing out of him but a maddening, "You'll see"—over and over.

We trekked across a long expanse of sand that filled my canvas exercise shoes and abraded my toes. We approached a grotesquely large American beach villa that I had previously taken into account in my daily jaunts. Built along the lines of a "stately" Georgian-style colonial plantation mansion, this pompous monstrosity could have been the Taj Mahal of some enfeebled tobacco grower with a preposterous name such as Lucky Chesterfield.

Fitzgerald remained thrilled by my obvious quandary. I had lagged behind, distracted by my thoughts about the building as I wondered what sort of man would have the egregious taste to conceive of such a thing as this. Who was he, really?

"Don't be a laggard!" F. called to me over his shoulder, waving me forward, as he was now keeping pace with Marion to avoid my inquiries.

Then, as we neared a long patio and narrow reflective pool, she rushed ahead, unaccompanied, and disappeared under a towering umbrella. Dogs yapped, so many moving about with such nervous quickness it gave me pause—these were the same species as the high-strung little bastard who had sampled my toe the other morning. But the hands belonging to a man with the blousy silk-clad legs sitting alone at the round table dropped some formidable scraps that kept the puny hounds at bay.

I moved up and got my first look at the man under the umbrella who was sitting next to the seat that Marion had grabbed. He was wearing collarless embroidered Chinese silk pajamas under an open plaid flannel bathrobe. He looked quite familiar. I felt as though I should know who he was. But what concerned me more was Marion's motive in introducing us to this fellow. If she was wealthy, it was nothing to be ashamed of. I could think of many uses for her money. But this contrived suspense was a totally inappropriate way to introduce me to her father, if that's who this was. I was disappointed in her for

"I MOVED UP AND GOT MY FIRST LOOK AT THE MAN UNDER THE UMBRELLA."

the first time, I realized—and a touch angry too. Mr. Fitzgerald seemed to know the man. He spoke even as Marion began her introductions.

"Hi, W.R."

"B-Bill, this is Scott Fitzgerald and Henry D-Duval. Gentlemen, Bill Hearst."

Mr. Fitzgerald stepped forward, cutting off my extended hand in his eagerness to get to the jowly, gray-haired old whale in silk brocade pajamas first. "Bill, how are you? We played tennis once at your chateau—Zelda and I were with Chaplin."

"You mean Casa Grande," Hearst corrected in a small, squeaky voice—incongruous for such a gelled mountain of a man.

"Yes, of course," Fitzgerald offered contritely. He seemed so anxious to please.

I was, too: "It is a distinct pleasure to meet Marion's father," I said with utmost cordiality—or so I thought.

Faces froze in weighted silence. "What's that?" demanded Hearst.

Fitzgerald whispered in my ear. "He's William Randolph Hearst, Henry!"

"Pleasure to meet Marion's *favorite*," I offered, thickening my accent in the hope that the old man would conclude I spoke his mother tongue with extra helpings of mush in my mouth.

He must have, for his grip became firmer then—thankfully. He tilted his sagging chin back and chuckled with a raucous trill, as if he were gargling with laughter. He blinked with uncontrolled self-consciousness as he met my eye.

"So, where ya from?" Hearst inquired of me.

"France," I said.

"Oh. Looks like ya got some trouble on your hands."

"It will soon be on yours and everybody's," I countered foolishly, realizing even as the bile passed my lips that such indignation is entirely inappropriate to my official position here—courting favor with influential fascists of the press such as he. It was a glaring mistake, one which I quickly attempted to undo. "It is a difficult situation for all of us—even the Germans. But I don't want to burden you with politics at breakfast . . . My, your estate is lovely."

"Thank you. Sit down and have something to eat."

We sat. An oversized plate piled high with steaming fresh hotcakes (those American crepes drenched in sweetened syrup culled from maple trees—I assume you've had them) was sitting in the middle of the glass-topped iron table. I was too confused to be hungry. Mister Hearst nodded at Fitzgerald, smiling with his nervous blinking eyes. "I enjoyed your recent performance."

Mr. Fitzgerald was perplexed. "I'm not sure I understand."

"Weren't you in that movie we screened just the other—"

"Scott's the w-*writer*, honey," Marion had to say.

"Oh, that's right. So, how's the writing game?"

Fitzgerald leaned forward in his chair, holding onto the edge of the table as if he wanted to push it into Hearst's chest. "Fine, fine, Bill. You should read a book sometime. They teach you things."

"Now, now," I said, trying to dispel the tension.

The old man pushed his chair back from the table with some effort. Half the dachshunds began wandering off, their keen instincts directing them to seek refuge from the impending storm. "Is that so?"

"Yes, it is. And, if I'm not the most important novelist in the world, I am still a writer. One would think that a man of your eminence could recall the road signs of culture, if nothing else."

"Well, well."

"My ass." Fitzgerald glared at him and got to his feet. "Think the Germans are as innocent as your cute little dogs? Look beyond the pretty trappings, why don't you."

Hearst turned to his paramour. "Is this for my edification?"

"You're damn right." Fitzgerald pointed an ever-chastising finger at the old lord. "If you try to keep the boys home again, like in the last war, you'll be hanging by your thumbs, I guarantee it, whether they go or not."

"Since you're such a brilliant political theorist, what would you suggest we do as a nation, Scott?"

"I'll tell you what I'd do—what Henry here and I are *going* to do."

I swept my arm across the table, knocking the plate of hotcakes to the pavement, along with my coffee cup and saucer. They shattered loudly on the cement, stopping Fitzgerald before he ruined everything.

"*Mon dieu!* I'm so sorry. Scott, help me pick this up."

Servants rushed forward to push us aside, even as Hearst informed us that we needn't bother.

"Shut up," I whispered in Fitzgerald's ear between my clenched teeth.

"So, let's have your brilliant theory, Mister Fitzsimmons."

"Fitzgerald, you old moron. You're too stupid to understand it."

Unwittingly, the uncultured fascist had come to my aid, as Mr. Fitzgerald angrily stomped off, heading back toward the soft warming sand.

I shook hands with Hearst, then I bowed over Marion's hand and kissed it as if it were her lips. "Writing is such a strain. I must go find my friend. It's been a pleasure making your acquaintance, sir. I will see you the next time you're at the studio, Miss Davies."

I must stop, Hy. My fickle flame Ava has succeeded in stirring up the poolside crowd. She and another strumpet (a shapely bucktoothed redhead) have perched themselves on the shoulders of two bronzed, sable-haired Tyrone Power lookalikes, and each is trying to push the other off. They topple off together every second or so and splash the rest of us; then the boys feel them up as they lift them back onto their shoulders. This letter is turning into papier-mâché.

To continue:

I bade Miss Davies and her old lord a politic adieu and went after Mr. Fitzgerald, who was already well ahead of me, having set off at a run to cool himself of his hotheaded, imprudent petulance. The tide was high, but he ran along the hard-packed sand on the shoreline, zigzagging left and right and attempting to dodge the jerky little breakers. I followed, bobbing in and out of my own thoughts as I tried to adjust to the suddenly altered image of the woman with whom I had fallen in love. I vacillated between scathing indictments and pea-headed rationalizations in an effort to comprehend both her deceptive misdirection and the fact of her long involvement with that nauseating old man.

How could she have ever done such things? She was a shameless scheming slut, simply lapping up whatever pleased her. I was the table scrap that came along one morning. *No!* I refused to believe it. The old man had killed her with kindness—that must be it. She was dying to get away from him and she was too ashamed of what she had let herself become to tell

5. This letter seems to follow in sequence and may have been written on the night of July 23, the same day. (ed.)

me who she really was. She wanted to be someone else—that was why she had contrived that persona. It was a necessary fiction (as was my own scenario writer alias), enabling her to snatch a few precious moments of respite from a tarnished burdensome existence. The poor, poor creature.

But why hadn't she used those same wiles to secure her independence from that despotic dilettante? Why? She hadn't wanted to, that was why. She'd do anything for a lousy buck. What made her any different from Ava, that easy lay from the hotel pool?

My mind was a shambles. Before I knew it, I practically ran Fitzgerald down. I stayed on his heels, then came up alongside him. Our shoes were soaked through; we sounded as if we were pressing grapes as we trudged along.

"I told him, didn't I?" Fitzgerald said, speaking cockily out of the side of his mouth.

"Almost . . . Thank God you didn't."

I was out of breath. My mind raced. To my infinite surprise, I had a hard time keeping up. I shut out everything the best I could, kept pace, then slowly lengthened my strides.

I moved like a machine then, good for any distance.

"Slow down," Fitzgerald panted.

"That's what I've been telling you! Pace—pace is everything, Sir. Jump ahead too fast and tell that man Hearst what we are going to do, and we would have been finished before we even started. Even if he had been sympathetic, which I doubt, our secret would have leaked to the wrong sources. He'd send cameras ahead of the Resistance just to make sure he covered the assassination."

"I doubt it," grumbled Fitzgerald.

"Think! The man is a yellow journalist. He cares nothing about you or your country—he just wants to make money. A fiery news item will do that for him."

"Don't *you* care about money, Henry?"

"Of course, I do."

"In a sense, he can't help it."

"What do you mean?"

"Money corrupts. He was born with two strikes against him."

"I wish I were so cursed," I said bitterly.

"You're lucky you aren't."

We had reached the pier, festooned with its somnolent, unlit Ferris wheel and merry-go-round, empty, closed, with no foot traffic for now. As is his wont, Mr. Fitzgerald stopped suddenly before I could anticipate his intention. I urged him on, but he screwed up his glance, mockingly eyeing me askance, as if to say the mere suggestion was too absurd to consider. I was too tumultuously tangled up in my own emotions to rest, so I continued, throwing off all reason as far as my purported reverence for pacing oneself. I sprinted like a panicked stallion giving his all, heaving his lungs out and spending himself before the wire.

I wound down and stopped before I got very far; then I walked back. I was preoccupied still with the notion of one of the world's wealthiest men contending with the "taint" of his money.

Mr. Fitzgerald sat on the dry sand, carefully watching a handful of the fine, hour-glass granules sift through his fist onto his palm.

"You mean to tell me you wouldn't wish that each of those tiny pebbles was a thousand dollars?" I challenged him.

He smiled sadly. "I'd rather have the rate of exchange for every cocktail I've imbibed."

"The point remains—if you were rich, you'd know what to do with it."

"Now, I would. But I've learned from setbacks and disappointments. Poverty has enriched me." He smirked. "Seriously, if I'd been born with it, I don't know."

"Look me in the eye and tell me you feel sorry for anybody who's got money."

He tried to keep a straight face, betrayed a smile, and then we had a laugh. Not that it did any good. I got carried away when we were sparring; then I hurt my back lifting the heavy dumbbells, as I tried to better fate or at least defy it enough to squeeze more truth from it than I probably deserved. After all, upon my first encounter with Miss Davies, I intuited that she was the sort of woman I tended to latch onto—someone avoiding something, seeking sanctuary and rejuvenation in a brief, frivolous affair. What a fool I was for trying to make it more than it could be. Why couldn't I leave well enough alone? Was I that lonely? Was it my ever-growing obsession with my suffering, vulnerable motherland, or Fitzgerald's fatalistic, infectious Keatsian romanticism that was transforming me from cynic to feverish idealist? Was it both? Was this state I was in a sickness or a cure?

Still unresolved in my relations with this haunting woman, I couldn't gauge myself and who I was or what I'd recently become without gauging her as she intended our relations to be now that we would both be changed with each other (or perhaps it wouldn't make much of a difference to her). I debated with myself through the afternoon and early evening, unsure whether I was deadlocked in a futile attempt to alchemize the sublime from dross pettiness, or if instead I would be shutting the door on something unique and wonderful if I were never to see the woman again.

I wasn't sure I wanted to. This phenomenon of love is dangerous. I felt weak. The day had been oppressively hot, but it was more than that. I'm embarrassed to say this, but I was slightly feeble-witted, as if I'd been wandering, lost. I kept losing the train of my thoughts. Later that afternoon, I found myself standing on the corner of Sunset Boulevard, with no idea how I'd got there or where I was going and why. I took a long moment to recollect that I was on my way out for lunch at the drugstore across the street.

After returning to the Garden of Allah after lunch, I was still suffering over matters when I heard my telephone bell from the shower. In my haste, I slipped on the tile floor, banging my left knee against the sink. When I entered the bedroom, the phone had stopped ringing. The silence was deafening. My nerves were raw—need I say more? I was getting hold of myself, deciding against this affair entirely, when the phone rang again, shattering my thoughts. I nearly jumped from the bed, then I grabbed the receiver.

It was her, of course. I forgot all my little reasons for breaking it off before she came to the end of her first sweet halting sentence. She had something urgent to tell me, but didn't want to say it over a party line. At her suggestion, we arranged to meet at one of her favorite places—the amusement pier in Santa Monica.

I wasn't sure if she suggested such a place because she presumed that, next to a movie, this would be the best entertainment for an uncomplicated person such as myself (something

I ordinarily enjoyed when I wanted to give myself a treat), or if she just wanted to impress me with how regular and easy to please a lady of her means could be.

I was not impressed, until, shortly after sunset, I saw her— until, weeping, she ran into my arms. And then the garish lights and giggling children eating fluffy pink candy clouds on a stick, the tattooed carney men beckoning one and all to play their rigged games, the hurdy gurdy and the roving harmonica and accordion players, the calculated, creaky metallic whine of the near runaway rollercoaster casting jagged Stegosaurus-like shadows, the joyous shrieks of those on the big ride—all of it was no longer base and common but sacred and forever beautiful.

Steady breakers thumped solidly against the pilings of the pier like a small boxer's hard little inside counter blows, pitting my heart against hers as we devoured each other with our anxious delight. My nostrils hurt with the musky, briny woman smell of the night sea mingling with the cloying scent of so much Lily of the Valley (her perfume), and the raucous carnival circled us, spinning its sweet, childish, pulsating, bright, innocent sin. Our love was a dizzy carousel, and the goofy siren call of a nearby calliope beckoned us to indulge without limit.

It is frightening to be so much in love, Hyman. Have I said this? What I see now, too, is that it is even more frightening not to be, if you are offered the rare opportunity.

But I'm getting ahead of myself. Marion was dressed rather simply in an obsidian-beaded gown laced with random jewels. Against the dark velvet of the larger night, her form was vague. What was visible shone with a spectacular effect that was no less than a legion of shooting stars. Her fingers sparkled with huge diamonds; her milky, delicately boned neck and collarbones were graced with the pride of ancient oysters. A diamond

tiara sparkled timorously through the soft spun gold layered
about her head. The truth was that she had tip-toed away from
a party—a rather large one, at her beach house. By the time
they realized she was gone, and the jealous old man had super-
vised a methodical search of all the rooms, it would be late into
the night. The evening was ours, she said.

There was much I wanted to say, but the crowded, rollick-
ing atmosphere distracted me. It wasn't until we had visited
half the games—shooting metal ducks with pellet guns, throwing balls in a barrel, and other such things—that the sadness
set in, for me at least. A blanket of melancholy settled on my
shoulders, bowing them with great disappointment in myself.
How could I have succumbed to believing in something that
shouldn't and couldn't happen? I had never thought of myself
as a weak man. But I supposed I was, at heart. I had found my
match—a woman who had held up a mirror to me. And oh,
what I had found.

Strangely, we had been standing in line for the rollercoaster
ride. (If you don't know, this is a sort of miniature thrill train
which runs over a ludicrous configuration of track in the manner
of vertical hills and valleys, and banked turns, and it goes at a
gallop. It's supposed to scare you—Americans like that. They
strap you in your seat!) The train returned with its most recent
crop of victims—some squealing with silly joy, but a few others
pale with regret now that they had tested their capacity for tor-
turous pleasure and found themselves wanting.

After we were locked in behind our safety bar in the first car
of the little wild train, and started off at a disarmingly slow gait,
I surmised we were in the roughest seats on the ride.

I had presumed we had something else to discuss, and I told
her so.

"D-do you hate me?"

Reduced to such elemental terms, my reason paled, even as we dropped off the peak of an unsettling incline. "Of course not, but . . ."

". . . then h-how c-could I have s-stayed with him?"

"Yes. That is exactly what I wanted to ask you.".

"I was w-weak, Henry. I thought m-money and s-stardom were everything. But now I know."

I find this very hard to tell you, but at that moment she pulled the diamond-studded tiara from the golden crown of her lovely head; in the same motion, she tore the priceless pearls from the shelf of her satiny neck. She tossed them both out into the night, over the water. I pulled my hand back as if to slap her face.

"Henry, w-what's wrong?"

The rollercoaster banked around a steep turn. I nearly fell out of the car. She grabbed for me, but I shrugged her off. "The money for those jewels could have bought guns."

"W-why would you w-want to do that?"

I realized what I was saying. "I mean you're a spoiled, wasteful woman to throw away so much money for which poor men would work their fingers to the bone."

The train raced down one final steep hill.

"Isn't love m-more important?"

"If you can both eat and sleep safe and sound."

"B-but love m-makes that p-possible."

We talked or argued until the ride ended and then was ready to start again. The attendant walked by and tipped his cap to Marion: "Hi, Miss Davies." So, she was a regular here. It was too late to get off. The train crept away for a second trip around.

She was hurt. Terrible tears streamed from her doe-like eyes.

"For your information, that was costume jewelry," she said in the cutest hurt voice. "Fake."

I couldn't stand it. Her spirit poured over me like honey.

"Oh, what are we arguing about!"

"I've n-never been w-wasteful—at least n-not for a l-long time," she pouted.

"I'm sorry."

"I w-was t-trying to t-tell you I love you." Little words are so important. Her stammer does that to me, makes me listen and cherish what would otherwise be obvious, but really is not— because of her, because of what she is to me.

"And t-that I'd d-do anything for you," she was still saying.

I told her I loved her and meant it in the moment.

We kissed rather long, then she told me that she'd always wanted to do "it" on "w-one of these."

I wasn't sure I understood—but then, quickly, I did. The thought of it—I can't tell you, Hy, how it excited both of us. It's a miracle we were able to manage, but I suppose we owe a great deal to that crazy toy train itself. Throttling up and down the breathless drops and inclines, fifty men, women, and children screeching with hysterical delight while she churned me into submission, her beaded gown draped about my lap, my arms encircling her. The two of us faced the boisterous night, pumping furiously, sweating so sweetly, hoarsely screeching our passionate moans over those of our fellow passengers. Riveted to each other, and delirious with all that is flesh and spirit, we dropped off the last peak of our quick, everlasting joy as the rollercoaster did the same. Then the ride was over. We couldn't stand. We went again, a third time, catching our breath, and praying silently, I think, that we deserved this much joy.

Why am I prattling on incessantly, sharing every detail of my love life with you? I feel guilty enjoying myself while others are suffering. This is why I feel compelled to let you know every little thing I'm doing. Rest assured, Hyman. I have not forgotten, and I will not let myself forget the larger scheme of things. It is just that now I find myself thinking slightly differently—a seemingly small change that, surprisingly, has affected me strongly. I am beginning to envision love and politics as inextricably intertwined. Love has plugged me into its special current. I am galvanized with a new sense of mission. In the past, I functioned employing my imagined, somewhat unrealized capacity; now, everything is tangible. I am a pursuer of life-affirming truth. I am a committed man in love with *one woman* and *one country.* So please do not worry, my friend. I may be in lotus land, but I am partaking of food of substance—and nothing else!

(unsigned)

PARAMOUNT STUDIOS

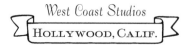

West Coast Studios

HOLLYWOOD, CALIF.

Telephone: Hollywood-2422 // Cable: FamFilm

July 27, 1940

Dear Hyman,

I am living in the pit of my stomach. I do not see how I can avoid getting bleeding ulcers from this, for never in my life have I been so torn. I am sure you have already read about it in the papers, but in case you haven't: our dear friend, William Randolph Hearst, who just yesterday was a frightened, fascistic isolationist with no interest in anything but the security of his unspeakably offensive assemblage of "artistic" loot stockpiled at his Castle in San Simeon, has suddenly changed his tune.

Three days ago, on the twenty-fourth—just a day after our catastrophic introduction at the beach—the old miser turned about entirely and voiced a startling change in policy regarding the war. In his own words, in the plain print of his very own normally boring column ("In the News") in the *Los Angeles Examiner*: "The entry of the United States into war may be considered more than a probability. In fact, it may be set down as a certainty." This will have a considerable impact on American opinion; it has already given an incalculable boost to British morale. I read today where the R.A.F. made leaflets quoting

Hearst's grand pronouncement and dropped them with their most recent bombs over Berlin.

I am weeping with happiness and despair. Happiness that miraculously, without compromising or sacrificing one stitch of our necessary security, Fitzgerald and I have shared a part in this—in moving mountains by getting through to that fat old slob. After all, there can be no doubt that we served as the instrumental catalyst that pushed the insufferable bore to get off his duff and think. We upset him greatly; Marion says so herself.

The despair is so hard to discuss, but I must try to get it off my chest. I will feel better, I suppose, if you tell me I have done the right thing. You see, I have been forced to end my affair with the only woman I have ever really loved. You are right that I am a forty-year-old man who sounds like an adolescent. But that is what this woman has done to me. I had to put a stop to it. Not because I wanted to, but her intensity left me no choice.

You are laughing, I am sure—for who am I to accuse her? If anyone lost sight of perspective and direction, it was me. I must have been mad to imagine that things could stay as they were, with regular morning meetings at the beach and the occasional rendezvous in the evenings. Two nights ago, she showed up on my hotel-room doorstep. I was worried for her and told her so. Mr. Hearst is an extremely jealous man. If she had stayed the night, the news would have ended up in the rival papers. Not only are the society columnists like Fitzgerald's Miss Graham (and many lesser lights) forever nosing about here, but they all have Garden employees on retainer. There would be a scandal. Marion would be humiliated, at least in Hearst's eyes—but what is worse, it could have a damning effect on his attitude toward the Allied cause. He could easily be provoked to turn against us in impotent childish vexation.

I got her to go home.

The next day, yesterday, she showed up at my Paramount office at noontime. After her departure, secretaries, writers, and even producers dropped by all afternoon, making wisecracks and insinuations. Her official explanation was that the two of us were meeting to discuss a new cinematic vehicle for her. This was her alibi if word got back to Hearst, and she tried it out on the handful of old acquaintances we came across around the lot. Walls have ears, and I had been afraid to stay and talk in my office. I was glad I had taken that precaution because our conversation was quite intimate. Luckily, I was able to steer her onto an abandoned Western set, where we had complete and utter privacy.

Our conversation was too searingly poignant to duplicate here in detail. Suffice it to say, Marion wanted to run away with me and would not accept anything less than my irrefutable, unequivocal agreement. I tried to reason with her, but without compromising my identity, it was impossible. I would not and *did not* tell her. The exchange was excruciating. Like a diligent homing pigeon, she persisted in returning to roost on the notion that writers can write anywhere. She has enough of her own money that we could live in style anywhere. She offered to finance my movies (based on scripts I have never written and would have no idea how to write), and then we could offer them to the studios for distribution, for a price. In the long run, this would be more lucrative. But in the longer long run (as I barely recalled, being in such a godawful quandary), the most crucial thing was our country's freedom. Hearst would never leave well enough alone if he knew what she was up to. He would humiliate us both and ruin us.

When I tried in vain to argue that it was just too difficult, she fell apart, convinced now that I didn't love her as she loved me. I insisted this wasn't true. Then, once she believed me, she told me she wanted to have my baby.

There was no way out, Hyman. I wanted to give her everything, tell her everything—even forget who I am and what I am really doing here. I had to let her go and I could only do that by alienating her; there could be no alternative without telling her about myself. I was playing with fire. If I told her, I could ruin both our lives. By virtue of our association, she could be tried in France now as a co-conspirator in a treasonous international crime, if matters got that far. Without jumping that far ahead, it was unfair to expect a highly visible woman such as herself—a woman many people recognized, and who was obviously overwrought—to remain silent about what L'Esprit Libre is planning. Beyond all this, there is the added wild card of Hearst's wrath and the multitude of harmful ways it could be expressed. Unequivocal love and devotion cannot prevail under such impossible circumstances.

I didn't sleep a minute last night. It took me until my drive to the beach this morning to know what I had to do. At first, I was going to tell her I was a spy for Hearst who had wanted to test her true mettle. But I couldn't—it might have been more than she could take. My cruel plan was this: I would ask her if I could borrow ten thousand dollars. She would agree. Pretending to be moved, I would confess I had to pay off an old gambling debt. Then I would leave a letter in plain view in the glove compartment of the Ford (easy to rig it to fall open)—a letter home to my French wife and children, the text of which would convey the happy news concerning the easy money to be picked up here in America. The text would also declare my absolute, unswerving love and adoration for this phantom family (the "only ones dear to my heart").

I picked her up at the beach and contrived a quick business stop at a non-existent producer's apartment to give her plenty of time. I bumped into the front fender on my way around the car and heard the glove box panel swing down.

It worked like a charm, Hyman. A charm. When I returned to the car, she was gone. I found the letter on the passenger seat.

I'll come back to her someday, if fate allows—though I don't see how we'll ever be able to build our romance back to the high place it was just a few days ago. I don't see how she could ever forgive me. I hate myself for this, but with the limited intelligence the good Lord allowed me, I just don't see what else I could have done.

I won't go on. I've given you enough of a headache for the time being. Still, though I'm sure I'm miserable company even as a pen pal, it's my deepest hope that I remain

Your friend,
Henri

Dear Hyman,

I'm sorry I have not been able to write. Putting words to paper does nothing but make me more aware of my situation. I've taken a liking to American whiskey, Dixieland jazz, and what they call big band music. I've grown fond of sitting in dark nightclubs, soothing my anxious heart with heavy drink and sad sonorous melodies, quelling or submerging my dull desire for what I know I can't have.

It's odd. I've never felt this way. Other women don't do a thing for me. Countless times, I've looked them over, undressing them mentally. In my mind's eye, I fill in all the blanks, see every silken contour, each sector of delight—yet I feel nothing. It's an exercise I perform to test myself, and I find it consoling that I never respond. I have enough problems to distract me at present—the last thing I need is to heap love on top of everything else. (I have the memory to cherish and shall use it like spiritual mortar in erecting our monumental plans for history.)

In the sharp, cruel light of morning, the things I don't like to think of come back to me, and the last thing I want to do is to write to you about them. Is it conducive to your health and well-being to hear how worried I am about our future? How nauseated I feel that a kangaroo court sanctioned by that moron Pétain and his hired puppeteers has found Charles de Gaulle guilty of treason and sentenced him to death (in absentia)? How tired I am of keeping up with this daily exercise regimen when I'm still queasy from my bout with bourbon the night before? How anxious I am about being told to write something at the studio now? And how difficult it is to be receiving Mr. Fitzgerald's generous assistance and fending off Miss Graham's increasing pique about the "unnecessary" amount of time he seems to be taking from their relationship to help his French friend? You don't really want to hear all of this, do you, my friend?

But if this unremitting chaos eventually results in the purpose that we have intended, then who am I to complain? When I say "chaos," I suppose I mean to address this stifling whirlwind of activity over the script I've been assigned. The studio morons and Fitzgerald are sucking the life out of me. I see buildings in my mind, not stories; things that are tangible and concrete. As push comes to shove with this bizarre process, I simply do not see how it's done. My immediate supervisor has told me to "dream up" a detective story set in Paris, with "lotsa murder and mayhem"—I don't even know what the latter word means!—"but always secondary to the romance angle." The studio has accumulated a great amount of recent European newsreel footage which with process filming on soundstages they hope to combine with original story material. "Absolutely no political angle," my supervisor says—they are going to edit out all stormtrooper footage and any evidence of carnage and destruction.

It's sickening, being required to frolic about the landmarks of the city dearest to my heart. A city that cries out its pain for all the world to hear—and I am supposed to shut my ears and eyes to it and encourage the rest of the world to do so, too. And if that is not bad enough, not only must I pretend to be happy and eager to perform this "precious" work, but I must show my boss what I'm writing as I proceed. I have become so nerve-wracked over this requirement, that, for the most part, I forget how offensive the work's premise is. I worry over creating some romantic tripe just to prove to myself I can do this thing—but I can't, Hyman. Writing fiction is impossible. What makes one approach to any story better than another? I am completely confused on this point. In architecture, you make new plans to improve on previous plans. You study your blueprints, you confer with your clients, you arrive at a result that will house a business or a family for as long as time allows (or until the Germans destroy it). But is the American lady brunette or blonde? Did she run away to Paris because she didn't love her husband or because her husband didn't love her? Or was it mutual? Or was it because she hit her head and became amnesiac and imagined she was a character from her favorite book?

In this script, the woman's husband comes to Paris to find her—therefore it should be his fault, says Fitzgerald. He should be guilt-ridden and eager to atone for something rotten he did. This must be Fitzgerald's guilt over his own marriage. He has indicated as much himself—which suggests that in each story the elements of theme and plot conform to the internalized obsessions of the writer's personal life. Mr. Fitzgerald is furious with such a view. He seems to think of his stories as versions of ideal Platonic forms dictating their own immutable components if one can only succeed in finding them. I'm not sure what I think, but either way, the writing isn't easy. I still feel foolish trying to do this thing. I have been spending the better part of every morning talking over the story with Mr. Fitzgerald while we exercise. He seems to know where it's going and doesn't mind doing all the work as far as determining a structure.

There is one rather big catch, though. Like a stern, patriarchal schoolmaster, he has the cheek to assign me reading. The Balzac and Maupassant are no problem, though I pay my secretary (a friendly spinster) at the office to do reports, for Fitzgerald quizzes me on what I'm supposed to have read and threatens to discontinue his much-needed assistance unless I earnestly submit to letting him play professor. I've pleaded that my facility with the Queen's English isn't good enough to enjoy reading much in that language (if the work in question isn't available in French). This has given me some justification for being behind on assignments. It would be impossible to keep up unless I were to pretend that I was in school—could you read *War and Peace* and *The Red and the Black* in one week, or even two? In addition to which I am writing most of the dialogue for my scenario at the studio during the day—with my secretary's help. "Please correct my English," I say. She polishes the male parts as I dictate, and I have encouraged her to play the heroine. Mr. Fitzgerald thinks her dialogue shows great promise, and I would tell her so, but now is not the time, as I am afraid that she would realize that she's doing most of the work. As things stand, she blushes upon my arrival each morning—clearly, she's smitten with me, though the poor thing's old enough to be my mother. Love is a cruel task-master taking hold of us at will when we least expect—as I well know. It hurts her, I can so easily see, but there's nothing I can do about it. I like her, I'm nice to her—but does buying her an occasional lunch or pastry mean that I'm encouraging her to be enraptured with me? Lest the deep well of her steady, patient passion run dry, I hope we finish this thing before she comes to her senses—but the truth, strangely, is that being fairly well read hasn't made it any easier for me to "dream up" this modern fairy tale. However poor or perishable the result, I must admit it is a talent to be able to do it at all.

The murder and "mayhem" are another matter. My supervisor and the producer now assigned to the project (entitled *Lost in Paris*) have decided that a dangerous killer should be on the loose, stalking Lillian, the heroine, as her husband is trying to find her. Women—at least two or three—who look like Lillian will turn up dead along the way. For the life of me I cannot understand why people seem to thrive on this sort of entertainment. Is man so primitive that he revels in bloodletting, celebrating his bloodlust imaginatively because society will not legally sanction him to vent his sweet rage? Yes, of course, yes. Hitler and Pétain are sufficient testimony to this sad truism. But it is a sick thing and I pity the impulse. I could never sit back and allow myself to be entertained by a "murder mystery." The desire for such fare seems to suggest an impotent simple-mindedness in those who are eager to be captivated by it; and ironically, these aficionados of manufactured murder and false fear would be the first to recoil before any real danger, even to the detriment of their own defense, and in so doing bring about harm to themselves and others.

This isn't just a theory, Hyman. I say this because I have recently killed two people—a man and a woman, to be exact.

Now that you've read that last sentence over for the third or fourth time, you've probably loosened your collar and broken out in a cold sweat, but please don't. If you're alarmed and wondering why I didn't say so right away (or cable to inform you), it is precisely because I do not want you to be unduly alarmed or fretful about the matter. A near disaster has been successfully averted. Of course, not being an experienced executioner, I was shaky and overwrought once the cushioning mantle of shock wore away from my inspired boldness and left me free to contemplate what I had done. My hand shook so badly for nearly two hours that I couldn't pick up this pen. It is for my own peace of mind that I have attempted to evince an air of equanimity or business-as-usual.

What happened is this: I returned from dinner last night and found the famous German émigré director Fritz Brunheimer going through my desk drawers. He is a resident of the hotel. I have seen him at the pool and the hotel bar before. Publicly, he has been an outspoken adversary of Hitler's Nazism. I know of him partially because he wrote and directed an anti-German movie I saw recently and admired, *Counterspy*, about an American spy who enlists in the Nazi underground after being seduced and brainwashed by a Mata Hari type. In retrospect, I see this film could just as easily be interpreted as subliminally suggesting that Germany is too beautifully seductive to resist. In the pat ending, the young man returns to New York and is discovered by his best friend, but there is an ominous aftertaste of countless other secret Nazis waiting in the wings for their big chance to take us over. I think Brunheimer took pleasure in making the German menace linger—for the man is a Nazi spy. Or at least he was.

When I saw him now, he smiled smugly, as if being kind enough to remind me that I was supposed to know him, and that he had only come here at my invitation to wait for my return. I was about to ask the obvious, when I saw that he had the letter I had begun to you. He had found my hiding place under the drawer's paper lining. The letter was sitting on top of the desk.

A short struggle ensued—I attacked him, and he nearly

stabbed me with a letter opener until I wrested it away from him. Finally, I was able to retrieve the letter and fetch my pistol from behind the nightstand. I held the gun on him.

"So zis is the way you vill greet someone looking for a writer?"

The bastard had the nerve to be indignant. Our conversation doesn't bear repeating, except to say he insisted he had come to offer me a writing job on a new picture he was going to both direct and produce. He said I had no right to threaten to shoot a man for being pathologically nosy.

I went through his pockets and found a handwritten copy of our code. The handwriting had a feminine slant.

At first, I had no idea how the man could have gotten ahold of this. The letter fragment was only a few sentences. He couldn't have gotten it from that. I kept the only copy of the code in my wallet. And I slept with that wallet under my pillow . . . except for the afternoon I'd met Ava Baker, Brunheimer's accomplice.

He denied it all, insisting that he had never seen the paper in question. Some sick person was trying to frame him for something he hadn't done.

"Here, in your country, they make scapegoats out of every German now. Please understand, it is as terrible as what der Führer is doing in my own homeland. I am innocent!"

"Oh, I understand, all right." I looked at the middle-aged weasel, with his pencil-line moustache, the brassy silk cravat tucked into a cheap, loud argyle sweater over outmoded knickers and burnished tan riding boots. "You look like a Nazi in camouflage to me."

We both laughed, for different reasons—Brunheimer, hoping to make light of a quickly darkening situation; myself, tearing my hair out for being a horse's ass, and straining to retain some semblance of calm and ascertain whether he had intercepted any of our other correspondence. But I had none of your letters (I burn them after reading them); also, I have mailed everything direct from the post office, during business hours. And no, I had not left an unfinished letter in my room since my first and only amorous interlude with Miss Baker—until tonight. Your whereabouts were safe.

Now, as for my own security, I wasn't sure. This cockroach's female counterpart had sought me out for a reason, obviously. If they knew I was an emissary from Pétain and Laval, that was one thing. But my affiliation with L'Esprit Libre was another, much graver issue—the difference between life and death for these vermin.

I nearly choked Brunheimer to death before he talked, begging for my mercy. He and Ava Baker knew nothing about me, apart from their orders to double-check my activities and report on me and the clandestine function of my position as assistant foreign affairs minister in the new Vichy regime. I had every right to communicate in code, and Brunheimer insisted he had neither remembered any part of it nor dispatched a copy to Berlin (not that it would matter if they hadn't gotten their hands on any other documents).

But I knew the kraut was just playing dumb. They thought they were onto something with me, they just weren't sure what.

Who else had they alerted? I didn't bother to ask. The only thing for me to do was to remove these obstacles, and then move on—let Mr. Fitzgerald remain behind until it became time, then rendezvous on target. Otherwise, there were sure to be others to pick up where Brunheimer and Ava Baker had left off. But I wasn't sure. Which would attract more attention—turning fugitive and fleeing, or staying?

Either way, if I didn't finish them, they would finish me. It wasn't pretty, heroic, or romantic. Scum that he is, Brunheimer turned on his partner, leading me to her on the condition that I let him go free. According to the worm, she masterminded their surreptitious activities, and blackmailed him into this against his will—I didn't ask him to elaborate, I simply nodded sympathetically, as if I already knew. Possessed with their last (and only) purposeful mission on this earth, they wept, pleaded, and carried on pitifully. Baker offered to be my slave for life, altogether forgetting Brunheimer.

Though they were convinced I was their stolid, determined executioner, I don't think I could have shot them if they hadn't run. We were in an orange grove under a full moon, in a section of the city called the San Fernando Valley where Brunheimer had directed me to take him. In another few seconds, the two of them would have disappeared under cover of the many lanes of thick, leafy trees. The fruit-bearing trees slightly muffled my four killing shots. You could barely hear the noise. It was as if a few pieces of gravid fruit had toppled to the hard ground.

Both had died with their eyes open. As I dumped them in the trunk of my car, they stared at me. I felt I was going to be sick, until I realized that this feeling derived from my fear of unexpectedly experiencing the same awful end—and with that, my nausea dissipated, and then vanished. I acknowledged that for me such an end wasn't unexpected but rather should be presumed—as inevitable as nightfall at the end of every day. That knowledge hardened me.

It wasn't the same for Mr. Fitzgerald, at first. When I arrived at his apartment, I had blood on my hands, and my shirt was soaked through with it. He was in his bathrobe and slippers. His eyes had that glazed, faraway look they get when he's been interrupted in his work.

"BOTH HAD DIED WITH THEIR EYES OPEN. AS I DUMPED THEM IN THE TRUNK OF MY CAR THEY STARED AT ME."

"I'm in the middle of something."

"Excuse me." I pushed by him, entering the apartment.

"Scott, who is it?" Miss Graham calling from the bedroom down the hall.

"Henry, I'm very—what happened to you?" He exclaimed with restraint, noticing the blood.

"I will tell you later. For now, a fresh shirt?"

I went to the kitchen sink and washed off as much blood as I could on myself. Fitzgerald brought me his shirt and I put it on.

He agreed to meet me down the block within a half hour.

I drove down the street, parked, and waited with the corpses of two Nazi spies in my trunk. The more I thought about them, the easier it was for me to accept having killed them in self-defense. They had been the aggressors in the service of their dread lord, the Führer. It was an eye for an eye, and each man for himself, as far as Nazis were concerned. They didn't deserve anything better.

Mr. Fitzgerald arrived at my car fifteen minutes later. He was in a tizzy, and fearful I had been wounded. No, the blood was related to something else. For some reason I couldn't then explain, it was imperative that I *show* him rather than say. But I had to offer some explanation, so I apologized for being vague, but said I couldn't talk about it just then.

He was quite fretful. "We're not in trouble, are we?"

"No. Not yet. But we will be."

"What does that mean?"

"This is a dangerous mission, Scott."

"I knew that already. We've discussed that a million times, haven't we?"

"Of course. I'm sorry."

We got in the car and drove in silence. When we reached the

coast, I began to prepare him. "Soon, you're going to be on your own for a while."

"How's that? You're not leaving, are you?"

"I must."

"Why?"

"It won't be for long, I hope. Pétain and Laval must think I'm still here."

"I don't understand."

I didn't answer him. I had realized the error in my thinking. If I were to leave, it would be tantamount to confessing to the murders and confirming my guilt regarding whatever other suspicions the Nazis might have about me. I had to stay put and bear up under their intense scrutiny. I couldn't be so frightened or overwhelmed with my own self-importance to believe that I was the raison d'être for the surveillance by Brunheimer and Baker. Surely, they had other enemies as well—others who would have relished doing away with them.

"Henry?"

"Yes."

"Relax. We're in this together, brother." Fitzgerald slapped me on the knee.

"I will stay as long as I can," I advised.

For one so lyrical in his prose, in conversation he can be surprisingly plainspoken. Thank God, really. It is tiresome conversing with people who talk like books. One senses that at heart they are not sure what they're talking about, and they try to make up for it by referring to other sources and putting on authoritative airs.

The moon was full and high like the whites of a virgin's eyes, we observed, comparing mental notes. Cars were parked along the seaboard as young couples tried to take advantage of the

pristine romantic glow of sea and sky, ever hopeful that the elements would conspire to trample caution and dull decorum and
evoke the sprightly sensual abandonment that every boy and
girl is living for in all their being—while the goods of flesh and
bone are new, and the inchoate mind (if there ever is such a
thing) is blessedly still unrestrained.

I spotted an unpopulated area—a narrow craggy palisade
just large enough for one car. I pulled onto the dirt shoulder at
an angle, with the rear end of the Ford slanted seaward.

Fitzgerald was nervous suddenly. "Why are we stopping
here?"

I'm embarrassed to think such a thing, let alone express it,
but from Mr. Fitzgerald's quick, sidelong glance, I had the distinct impression that he was fearful, momentarily, that I had a
disguised motive in stopping here—an amorous secret which,
to his horror, I was on the verge of daring to declare to him.
How could such a thing have occurred to him? Perhaps it's a
longstanding problem of his. Or perhaps it's the cultural difference causing either of us to misread the words, motions, gestures, social conventions of the other.

I got out of the car quickly and walked around to the rear
and opened the trunk.

"It *is* beautiful," Fitzgerald was saying. He had stepped out
of the car and was standing at the edge of the cliff, looking out
over the water. He lowered his voice and declaimed some verse
in a deeper, professional-sounding voice—a sonnet about a
mania shared by miners, astronomers, explorers, and writers for
discovering new truths in the forms of precious gems, comets,
fountains of youth, and stories.

"Yes. So true," I said. "The quest is such hard work but so
rewarding ultimately—even with the necessary terrors which

emerge from probing the dark depths of the unknown . . . Come here, Scott."

He gave me that look again, then his brow furrowed stoically, his lips pursed with discernible distaste, and he approached me, moving stiffly, composing himself with a certain wooden determination, in case he had to think fast and defend himself against any irregular behavior on my part. As he neared, he looked me in the eye, staring manfully at me as one soldier to another, and suggesting, I suppose, that I remove whatever foolish thoughts I might possess from my mind immediately.

"Help me," I said, nodding toward the two corpses in the trunk. Tousled and tumbled about from the drive, their heads were now side by side. Their eyes were still open, and the moonlight caught the dead orbs in its path, illuminating them with a sick viscous limpidity. You didn't have to see their dark, blood-matted hair. You could tell they were dead immediately— there was a fishy glaze to them, as if they were a couple of trout laid out on ice in the market.

Fitzgerald had caught the direction of my gaze. What he saw dropped him to his knees, his hands latched onto the Ford's rear bumper to break his fall. Quickly, he glanced up at me in disbelief. Then he raised himself from his knees and peered in at the corpses once more.

There was anger in his eyes now as he turned to me again. "That's the director, Fritz Brunheimer, and that girl you met at the Garden. You—you killed them, Henry!"

"They were Nazi spies, Scott. They were trying to break my cover."

"Fritz wouldn't hurt a fly. I've known him for years."

"You *thought* you knew him. I caught the man reading my

mail in my room. His partner had stolen a copy of my correspondence code."

Scott had gotten to his feet. He glanced back at the corpses once again. His jaw fell a notch and started quivering. He turned away and retched.

"He was broke," Fitzgerald said, without looking at me. "He had two ex-wives."

I lost my restraint. "This is exactly what I wanted to see. It's why I waited to show you instead of telling you at your apartment or in the car. I wanted to test your reaction. And I must say it is a good thing I did now rather than later. First you are angry with me because I have killed these . . . monsters. Now you're making excuses for them? The man needed money—so it is all right he became a Nazi? Why not rob a bank? That would at least make him an honorable criminal. And what leads you to believe his Nazism was a recent development? I bet that piece of shit was a Nazi years before he came here. He was probably a Nazi before they called them Nazis. DO YOU HEAR ME, MISTER FITZGERALD?"

He stood there, dumbfounded.

I continued. "Good. I think you're beginning to understand. Not that it makes a difference. You've gotten a small firsthand taste of the terror of war. So now you can lock yourself in your little apartment and write about it. I'd rather have you do that than panic later—when I will need you. And I do not condemn you. Writing, I suppose, is a form of bravery, too. Not all of us must be courageous warriors. Not that I am myself—but I will do what I need to do. I know I can do that much. It is just a lucky thing you didn't see the action of battle when you enlisted in your youth. We might have lost our chance to read your marvelous stories—I mean that. Dying in battle or losing one's nerve in it are the same thing. They can ruin a man for life. You're lucky."

"How so?"

"That it didn't ruin you. You were able to build your self-esteem as an artist and write your fiction."

"Fuck my fiction."

"No. Do not say that."

"You're saying I never would have been a writer if I had had to fight."

I shrugged. "How should I know? I'm upset a little, I guess. Please, I am sorry."

"I'm still in," Fitzgerald insisted.

"You should think this over," I suggested, baiting him. "You may make your contribution by staying home. War is a disgusting, vile business. Thousands of innocent people are being trampled, mauled, and slaughtered by the Nazi machine every day. One must meet such evil with a sort of evil of one's own. Your blood must turn cold and yet stay warm at the same time—so you can remember *why* you are turning yourself into a monster."

"I know," Fitzgerald said, nodding.

"This mission will be achieved with or without your assistance. I have alternate plans. I do want to push you into this, but not to the point of courting failure for you and all of us concerned."

"I WANT TO DO THIS!" Fitzgerald screamed.

"Good," I said, finally. "Then help me with these bodies, please."

(unsigned)

Hollywood, California
August 16, 1940

Hyman,

If I seem to have gotten carried away with the drama of it all, I apologize. My only excuse is that my waking life presently revolves around concocting plot lines for this silly mystery-romance I have been working on.

I'm not used to this sort of thing. I'd never dream of spending my time this way. I live in a sort of waking dream, and this storybook-land existence usurps my thoughts to the extent that what is real in my life doesn't seem that way anymore. Things are becoming blurred at the edges, less sharply defined. I know what we're going through might be construed as an adventure— though hardly worth celebrating, as it is motivated by the unjust suffering of so many people. Still, unaccountably, I feel as if I am a stranger looking on at myself. Though I have employed numerous guises to protect both myself and our common cause, I had not felt the least bit distanced from myself and my task until now. I don't know if it is just that time is catching up with me as I accumulate these odd experiences, or whether the writing has exerted some undue influence on my imagination—but it's not good. I find that I am beginning to worry without reason.

I should be concerned, even vigilant—yes. In the past I may

not have been sufficiently. But now I worry about everything. Waiting to hear from Pétain and his boy Laval is getting to me. I can't take it sometimes. I see my hand start to shake when I light a cigarette, and I wonder when and where I'll be able to sneak my next drink. This writing is for the birds, Hy. No wonder writers are difficult high-strung characters (journalists like yourself excepted, of course). It's this constant weaving of tall tales—it gets the better of you, Hy. You get overstimulated in your fantasy life. You start to see and suspect things that may not be so. You begin to get more wrapped up in what you think and feel than in what is. You become overly self-involved; your perception becomes distorted.

For instance, I know I must be on guard—"on the lookout," as Mr. Fitzgerald has said—now that I've taken care of those two Nazis. Surely there are others on their trail who will pick up where they left off. I must be watchful, I know, but it has been less than ten hours since Fitzgerald and I dragged the bodies from the trunk and dropped them over the cliff. I doubt if anyone's found them yet or even suspects they're missing. But I am like a lunatic, Hyman. Don't laugh, but I think everyone I see is a Nazi. When I picked up the morning paper on my doorstep, the bellboy passed by, carrying a breakfast tray. He merely tipped his head and waved, as he always does—but suddenly I didn't like it. I frowned and turned away, hurrying back into my room. He's a good-natured, chipper little hustler—slightly seamy maybe, but not a Nazi spy. He's not sharp enough or sly enough. He's a middle-aged man who steals the maids' tips.

Speaking of maids, these tired, expressionless washer-women also are suddenly appearing devious and sinister—as if those plain looks are poker faces concealing a trick card up all their sleeves. The desk clerk smiled at me and asked me how I was doing when I came into the lobby to check my mail. "Fine," I said, guardedly. He seemed too friendly. The waitress at Schwab's Drugstore asked me what I did last night. I panicked, forgetting this was our usual banter when I visit the lunch counter. She flirts with everybody—it passes the time for her. But before I could stop myself, I asked, "What makes you so interested?"

"Gee, bub," she snapped back, "ya better have a bromo for that hangover." She gave me the cold shoulder, and I did my best to make amends, borrowing the excuse she offered. Still, even as I apologized, I found myself studying her in a different light. Everybody has an ulterior motive to me now.

I'm nervous that people are going to start wondering what I'm so nervous about. On the surface, I'm doing quite well. I received a raise in salary last week, as a matter of fact, and they moved my secretary and me into a bigger office.

I don't have to be nervous about Mr. Fitzgerald, at least. My sore jaw just reminded me of another thing I should mention regarding last night's activities. I won't bother you with every bloody detail, but it did take some doing to prepare the corpses before we disposed of them, tying one with a wheel rim, the other with the jack and car tools, to weigh them down. Fitzgerald assisted—his face frozen into a mask of grim determination. Understandably, it was an ordeal for him. It's not every day one wraps up a couple of dead people to be delivered onto the rocky shores of eternal oblivion (hopefully). Be that as it may, I wasn't ready to leave well enough alone yet. I continued chipping away at Fitzgerald, gauging his muster and true capacity. I deliberately got on his back during the drive home to Hollywood. The silence preyed on me, I suppose, as neither of us had spoken for some time. I was, I will admit now, nearly as jumpy as he was.

We headed up the winding canyon road from the coast. The thick briny sea air thinned into a more vernal blend of eucalyptus and sage, and just a touch of that intoxicating, candy-flavored, night-blooming jasmine. No one on the road. Unbearably peaceful. I turned to Mr. Fitzgerald and told him it was plain to see that he needed a drink. Was he sure he was going to be able to stay on the wagon? I might have asked the same of myself, Fitzgerald suggested, informing me that his sensitive olfactory faculty could detect a drop of the cursed elixir from a mile away.

I baited him. "You're imagining things."

"Imagine this!"

Quick as a cat, a fist—his right—traversed the dark and detonated into my cheek and jaw like a stick of dynamite. Luckily, there was no traffic and I was heading uphill. I blacked out for a second or two, waking to find Fitzgerald's hand on the wheel and the Ford stalled and rolling backwards.

Through a fog which I suspected wasn't entirely natural, I heard him querying me in a worried voice. "I'm sorry, Henry. I don't know what got into me. Are you all right?"

Could I truthfully be angry at such a forceful, authoritative blow? It was indeed an honor to be knocked silly by one who just a short while ago would have been hard-pressed to stun a fly or hold his hands up unassisted. Thus, as the cobwebs cleared from my head, I was assaulted by my own spontaneous glee. I leaned back and laughed heartily to the high heavens.

I started up again and resumed driving. I assured Mr. Fitzgerald it was all right, and even went so far as to pat him on the back.

"That was something," I told him. I moved my jaw. Thankfully, it wasn't broken.

Our short, intensive sweaty regimen has paid off. Mr. Fitzgerald is in shape now, I'm proud to say. The proof is in this sore jaw of mine. I'll wear the bruise proudly.

All my best,
Henri

P.S. Have you received my telegram? Wire me back on which alternative code you would like to implement.

Hollywood, California[6]
August 26, 1940

Dear Hyman,

It is 3 o'clock in the morning, and as my head is swimming in a sea of scotch, I cannot lie down in the dark and close my eyes (even though I know I am tired enough to sleep like the dead). It makes me too dizzy—and besides, I always get a worse hangover if I go to sleep before I've sobered sufficiently.

I shouldn't be telling you this, of course, and you know I wouldn't if I thought I had a serious problem with liquor. I couldn't write at all in this blasted-bitch, headache-inducing new code of ours if I were degenerating into your average stumblebum drunk. Let's just say I'm soaking my sore toe so I can keep putting my shoe on. Whether it gets better or not, I can live with it if I must, with or without the Epsom salts (an American soaking curative—try it for sore bones in your bath).

I've been meaning to write you anyway, and since my tongue and pen are feeling thoroughly unfettered, let me just say the last letter I received from you prompted much thought from

6. An entirely new codal language is introduced at this point, one of considerable complexity which resisted the transcriptive talents of numerous linguistic experts for many months. See Harold Isaacs, "Breaking The Duval Manuscript," *Journal Of Contemporary Linguistics*, June (1983). (ed.)

my somewhat addled brain. Let me get to the thesis here. Not that you asked (though I don't feel you would have gone to such lengths in describing the situation—and her, particularly—if you were not soliciting my opinion), but the answer is no. I do not think you should get involved with that woman. NO!

"Who are you to say?" I'm sure you're saying. "What could *you* possibly know about love?" Not much, I'll allow. I'm the first to admit that my changed attitude to the fair sex has yet to be tested by the debilitating rigors of time and tempting opportunity. But whether my current state of mind endures, you are lovingly enmeshed in a different set of circumstances. Think of your wife and children, Hyman. You're jeopardizing the ever-precarious sanctity of all you hold near and dear. "She will never know," you reason—but not so, my friend. Let me share a deep-seated conviction: any woman of average intelligence is easily capable of divining whether her husband has remained faithful to his matrimonial pledge. If she has been faithful herself, it will be second nature to her. She won't have to know any details—she'll just sense it, her nostrils flaring with a nondescript, maddening scent. Suddenly she'll pounce on you, eating away at your insides until you confess gladly and abjectly beg for her forgiveness, feeling confident that your transgression will be quickly forgotten. But again—not so, my friend.

Yes, she will find out—take my word for it—and your home life will never be the same. Your children will lose their respect for you. And then she will either divorce you or make you a public cuckold, flirting with the world in front of your face— well, not Marguerite, if I know her at all, but the sacred trust between you would be irreparably violated.

You must make every effort to resist carnality's pernicious lure. Just because I have been a pig (and don't forget I have always been unmarried!) does not mean that you must follow in my footsteps. I see you and Marguerite as France itself. Let us not fall prey to degenerative influences, please (I don't mean to parody Pétain here). After all, look where my dalliance at the hotel got me—my god, the strumpet was a Nazi. Isn't this God's way of telling me I should cleanse myself?

Don't fall, Hyman! It's a long way down. I realize you're terribly bored there in Washington, and I don't want to lecture you, but there are too many matters more important than a fine piece of ass right now. So she has nice legs and the breast of a dove—so does your wife, who I'm certain is more of a woman. These American women, with few exceptions, seem like mules. Lovemaking, for most of them, is like packing a heavy uphill load. They carry their burden until the rider reaches his destination, then wait for a handout—hoping it's a diamond or a nice home. Sex is a means to an end—they don't really like it. This is why most rich and powerful American fellows have European girlfriends.

Things will get better soon. We can't sit here in America forever. Hollywood, for me, after two months, is now no more exciting than a back alley in Pigalle. The people are so mentally primitive. The only thing anyone wants to discuss is how much money he has or will have, or how much some undeserving third party has gotten his sticky hands on. And these aren't shopkeepers, streetwalkers, or clerks! This is the supposed American intelligentsia—leaders in the popular arts. God, do they bore me!

And they're nervous, too. They can't converse because they're always in a hurry—as if someone is following them or they need to relieve themselves. They know nothing of the art of conversation. It's almost as if their anxious eyes are telling you that something terrible will happen to them if they stop and talk a minute. In all my life, I have never met such dull and inarticulate people as the busy little bees I encounter daily at the studio—buzzing nowhere to no avail. They'll never make honey, even if they're supposed to, since none of them trusts his instincts enough to know where to find the nectar. I've altogether given up trying to talk to them. I'd sooner write you a letter or talk to my shadow on the wall. There's nothing so depressing and disconcerting as attempting social intercourse with a truly uninspired human being.

What excuse does any man or woman have for not exulting in whatever scrap of life they can? Please do not think I am skipping rope like a child. It is just that I cannot help but savor my freedom as I reflect on what is happening to the British now. I wept with joy at the news that the RAF is bombing Berlin; but as for France itself, I feel the same as when I was in mourning for my mother. Thank God she didn't have to see or experience these times. She despised herself enough for disavowing her Jewish heritage, but she always said it was worth it to give my brother and me a better life. We all know what that honorary Nazi Pétain means when he urges the "purging of our administration, into which too many newly nationalized Frenchmen had inserted themselves." He cannot be up to any good regarding either the refugee situation or Jews in general. The long-lost Jew in me feels it in my bones. I guess it depends on how Vichy will define "newly nationalized." If that means anyone whose heritage has not been completely French for at least a thousand years, French Jews are going to be in serious trouble.

Enough headaches for now. I must get to sleep. It's after four and I must be ready to canter a few kilometers in two hours, when Mr. Fitzgerald is going to pick me up. We have been driving together to a nearby lycée, where we run on the track. Going to the beach takes too much time; besides, I do not want to run into you-know-who. Fitzgerald is gaining strength while it seems I have been deteriorating. (I'm afraid I have gained weight!) He has just gotten a new scenario job, to adapt into movie form a stage play about an alcoholic actor—a subject he should know well. He carries on so in either elation or despair, he's nearly an actor himself.

You should have seen him when he was out of work for a few days. It wasn't as if he had been fired. He had finished his last scenario job based on his short story "Babylon Revisited," and within hours he turned into a sullen, morose character who believed that the world was entirely against him because he had been gauche and flamboyant and devoid of all social conscience in the boom days of the twenties. He thinks he's a symbolic figure of wasteful extravagance, and that most of the cognoscenti wish he was dead. This may not be far from the truth, and we can use Fitzgerald's self-doubt to our distinct advantage, as I've said before. But for the moment he is happy because his salary for the next few months will be $1000 per week. When he's feeling flush and triumphant, he picks up the check when we eat out, of course. And the most trivial events—such as the busboy possessing the same Christian name as his—are interpreted as being terrific omens boding great renewed fame and fortune for him.

Do you feel that it's normal for a man to be this extreme? I suppose, considering that he's a writer, certain allowances must be made. But you're a level-headed man, Hyman. You've never carried on so. Can there be such a dramatic difference between fact and fiction writers? Or is Mr. Fitzgerald just the odd man out? He is *not* very emotionally dependable. The worst thing about this is that when he's glum, he becomes indifferent about both his fate and that of the world (the day before his latest assignment came through, he called me at Paramount and announced that Hitler rose to power on the wings of a massive popular reaction to the international Jewish communist conspiracy, which was nothing more than a cover for the powerful financial interests of the Jewish plutocracy). I laughed at first, thinking he was joking. "Shut up!" he screamed, hanging up. That's when I realized he had been serious in this delusion. We have since discussed his love-hate relationships with his many Jewish friends. It was at that point I felt compelled to inform him that I myself am Jewish. This seemed to confuse him at first. Ultimately, however, I think my little revelation inspired him to decide that some Jews can be human. All I know is that he has made no further antisemitic proclamations to date in my presence.

Enough. I must sleep. I pray he doesn't lose this job or get depressed again, given all the other problems with which I must contend. I'm not a doctor of the mind.

(unsigned)

October 8, 1940

Dear Hyman,

How much longer can we sit here and rot? Aren't you sick of chomping at the bit? I haven't heard anything from either Laval or Pétain.

No one has responded to my intelligence reports in over a month. It's not that they had been trumpeting my praises, but I had been receiving communiques that at least acknowledged receipt. I haven't had much to tell them: "F. has clearance from *Life* magazine. Stop. Date?" They're probably confused because Britain refuses to roll over and play dead, like we did so gamely. (It may become necessary to begin hedging bets between the two possible victors, in the unlikely event that the Brits end up surprising everybody.) Either that, or Vichy has pulled the plug on me because of the successful enemy intelligence penetration we may have incurred in August.

I am not really worried about the second possibility, however, since it seems that, had they known, I would have been disposed of weeks ago. This gives me renewed confidence. I just wish I could say the same for Fitzgerald. We are at odds on the refugee issue. I'm afraid this may be his delayed traumatic reaction to my involving him in dispatching those two pests.

As for myself, I have come to my senses, I suppose, regarding the possibility of Nazi infiltration here in Hollywood. There is not much of it, I can see now. This interminable sojourn has slowly baked my nervous system into a foundation of cement—it was either that or complete collapse and panic, so it wasn't as if I had a choice. On the other hand, Mr. Fitzgerald is in a state of constant nervous agitation. He doesn't like to be working on a book, scenario, and stories all at the same time. But that doesn't explain his poor judgment in being so damn suggestible to the fifth column propaganda scare that America's wily anti-Semites have been working up. Since these bigots allege that a large percentage of the refugees may be disguised Nazis, the American public is urged to do everything in its power to avoid risking the compromise of its national security by allowing almost nobody to enter the country.

This is how their thinking goes, and Mr. Fitzgerald has fallen in with them. He does not see that what happened in August was due to exceptional circumstances. He continues to insist that it's all a Nazi plot and that every refugee who enters this country could be a Nazi spy. This is just what the hatemongers would like all Americans to believe. It goes without saying that America must be vigilant; but if this country refuses to open its doors (even temporarily, until the Nazis can be stopped), then it, too, is collaborating with the enemy.

Fitzgerald has said I'm crazy. I think he's begun to doubt the mission again. In voicing his confused thoughts, more than once he has asked me whether my interests lie with the Jews or with France. And what would you say, my friend? "They are with both, you moron," I told him proudly. "And the world, too—that is, America and any other countries that are still free."

I can't stand the sight of him anymore. I haven't talked to him in two days, and I must say I feel like a new man (getting away from him has a rejuvenating effect on me!)—almost well enough to go through the motions with him once more, as I know I must if I want him to keep his big Irish mouth shut. I'm finished with that story my secretary wrote for me. I helped her buy a new car ($75) to express my appreciation, but I feel I learned enough during the enterprise to be ready if they ask me to write something else. In fact, I miss not working on the problem of a story. There is something somewhat mathematical to it—like planning a plain building—at least the way they do it here. After all, it is the motion picture *industry*.

And don't worry, Hy. I will never breathe a word of what we've discussed to Marguerite. I understand what it's like to be lonely. We're animals. We need warmth. If that sounds insulting, I don't mean to be. I just don't know how else to put it. Marguerite may be lonely too. Whatever happens, when the two of you are reunited, you'll forget everything else. That's the way love is, isn't it? The one we cherish bullies the also-rans out of the way—though when the cat's away, the mice will play, eh? Sorry.

It's just that true love is such an enigma.

Henri

Hollywood, California
October 13, 1940

F. Scott Fitzgerald c/o Henri Duval
(delivered by classified courier)

October 12, 1940

My dear Mr. Fitzgerald:

An invitation has been extended to France to meet with der Führer. As this momentous occasion will undoubtedly leave an indelible impression on world events, it is in the vital interest of France, and all nations interested in promoting a lasting peace, that we solicit your attendance as an ambassadorial press representative for the United States of America, so that this auspicious event may be carefully and accurately documented for our American friends.

So much is at stake—the goodwill of your country is inextricably linked to restoring global equanimity and a spirit of international cooperation that will stand the test of time.

The exact date, time, place, and all related final arrangements will be cabled directly to the US State Department. A district representative should be contacting you shortly to apprise you of all last-minute particulars. You may request that the marshal's acquaintance, Mr. Henri Duval, accompany you as escort and translator, if you like—although we are not sure if this will be allowed. France assures him diplomatic immunity and complete egress if both he and the proper American authorities should decide that his presence for the occasion will expedite matters to the satisfaction of all concerned.

Perhaps our prayers will be answered, and an interim peace will be achieved, so that Mr. Duval and others in similar situations will be able to return home during the war if they so desire. This is one of our basic goals. Is it too much to ask?

We will look forward to making your acquaintance.

Yours truly,
Philippe Pétain

We didn't expect to have it cleared this way through open channels, of course. At first, I was terrified, especially when half the State Department and the FBI jumped us within an hour of my receipt of the letter. Two quiet men took us to a grim little building and placed us in two small, stale, connecting rooms with but one tiny window (closed). They grilled the two of us together and separately. Not that either of us has slipped, but they're sure I'm a mole for Vichy—though they don't seem to care, as I think Mr. Fitzgerald has done a credible job convincing them that he's going to share whatever intelligence he gets from the trip.

My inquisitor did the logical thing of continually circling back to the genesis of this proffered arrangement to clarify the "small points." He didn't seem like much in his poorly pressed plain blue suit and irritating black tie, until he commenced his formal inquiry in a gentle voice, to avoid detection by his colleague and Fitzgerald in the adjoining room. It was oddly

"THEY GRILLED THE TWO OF US TOGETHER
AND SEPARATELY."

humorous, at least at first. His looked impassive, at best, and his neck and shoulders were formidably oxlike, but this infernal voice of his was like that of an ingenuous teenager trying to perform hypnosis. Maybe he was, but I kept my wits about me enough to persist in telling him that Mr. Fitzgerald and I had met at the Garden of Allah, that I had served under the marshal, evacuated at Dunkirk, and emigrated to the US to seek work in my profession until I could return to France. Mr. Fitzgerald had wanted to cover the war and asked me if he might write the marshal and request an audience to discuss the pressing issues of the day. Knowing that the marshal has always been an ardent admirer of many things American, but never imagining that the marshal himself would ever receive Fitzgerald's missive (much less respond to it!), I told him to do as he pleased. The rest is (or could be) history.

Fitzgerald told me they want to know whether France is going to remobilize with Germany to extinguish Great Britain. No surprise they're curious, as the US would be the next to go. (This is not information for consumption by the public, and F. is a little perturbed on this score; heretofore, he has always written for publication and an audience of thousands. His readership for whatever he writes on this conference will consist of a handful of bureaucrats who will want nothing more than to debrief him upon his return and take notes on whatever is politically relevant.)

I think they are going to let me accompany Mr. Fitzgerald. They probably intend to deport me, and this is the easiest way to do it and gain some intelligence at the same time. Vichy must have had this figured. There's no way the Americans couldn't suspect something fishy with me, although there's also no way they could resist taking advantage of this golden opportunity. Is Vichy banking on getting F. to take home a message in a bottle—one that will make the mad Führer goosestep with delight?

I can't write any more for now, as I know half the city's following me—and we know I'm not dreaming anymore.

Henri

Hyman,

I may be writing this letter to myself as I am not sure it is safe to send you anything now. I've just seen the text of Pétain's latest pronouncement ("France is prepared to seek collaboration in all fields, with all neighbors") from October 11. No wonder the State Department is anxious to send us on our way. We leave for New York tomorrow morning.

I think that Mr. Fitzgerald has taken command of the situation. I wouldn't dare tell you all the crazy things I have said and done over the last forty-eight hours, but suffice it to say—for the moment, at least—Mr. Fitzgerald has become a rock. His newfound confidence is unshakable so far, and now *he* is the one tossing out *my* bottles! I had a difficult time last night, Hyman. The State Department representative took us out for dinner, and my sense of being scrutinized from afar but close at hand—someone always looking over my shoulder—nearly got the better of me. Something in me is dying to scream out "We're on the same side—I, too, want LIBERTY!" and be done with it. I want someone (anyone!) to share in my responsibility. I'm crying out in the night . . .

NOOOOOOO I'm not. I'm calmer now. Yes, I am, really.

But I began sobbing at the dinner table and I couldn't stop. I'd laugh hysterically in between the tearful jags as I vainly tried to impress our host that I was enthralled by something unbearably funny I'd overheard at a neighboring table.

"News from home," Fitzgerald explained tersely for the man's benefit.

The taciturn fellow nodded, slowly. "I see," he said.

I nodded as well. Our host ordered champagne. Mr. Fitzgerald covered his glass before the steward could pour. I was next. I clenched mine and lifted it in prayer.

"Henry, you said you'd help me pull my wagon." I looked at Fitzgerald who smiled with impish pathos.

"Oh, yes, Scott. That's right."

One more drink at that point and I would have been finished. Fitzgerald was a genius to see it. I was bad enough when we went bowling later with the State Department man and the two fellows who had given us our grilling the other day. Though I had never bowled before, I took to the sport with a fiendish combativeness. I became angry with myself every time my beginner's luck lapsed and I rolled a "gutter ball" (sending the bowling ball into the gully on either side of the long varnished lane—thus missing entirely the ten big-bottomed, roly-poly bowling pins, which seemed to chuckle at me for being so artless as to think I could knock them over). Within a short time I was egregious company—demonically sullen, brooding, awful. I retired to the bar where I drank a dozen cocktails of every description, and then I lost my head, I guess, when the bartender left for a moment. I began pounding and kicking at the bar, screaming inanities: "Where are you when I need you!" You see, metaphorically, the bartender was America, and I was France. He wasn't there when I needed him.

Fitzgerald got to me first. He shook me and shook me. As I said, I'm calmer now. We're leaving in a few hours. Everything is going to be all right.

Better to panic in a restaurant or go berserk in a bowling alley bar than to succumb to weakness at the decisive moment. I pray I have gotten all the cowardice out of my system. Mr. Fitzgerald has recommended that we read a novel called *The Red Badge of Courage* together. Not that I mind, but I think we're going to need a lot more than a good book to guide us.

Goodnight, Hyman. Thank you for being so patient with me.

Sincerely, I am proud to be—

Your friend,
Henri

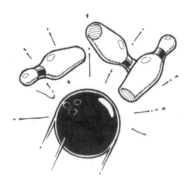

◇◇

October 18, 1940

Dear Hyman,

As you can see from the stationery, Mr. Fitzgerald, Alan (the State Department representative), and I have taken rooms here at the Hotel Algonquin. Fitzgerald has prattled on quite a bit about the hotel's great literary history. It seems that a group of poets manqué met here on a weekly basis to beg for alms in the form of whatever potent libations they could wheedle from any unsuspecting out-of-towners they could beguile with their inferior poesy. They became popularly known as Manhattan's Merry Men. Few achieved even a modicum of literary success—then the stock market crash brought on the Great Depression, the hotel trade tapered off, and the Merry Men lost their adoring audience.

It was then, tragically, that a few formed a daisy chain on the Algonquin roof and did a little jig off the edge that once again made them eternal[8]. Financial disaster is not funny, really—

7. Encoded script on hotel stationery. (ed)

8. Duval (or Fitzgerald) is a veritable fount of misinformation. The group was called the Algonquin Round Table, and it consisted of many of the most successful playwrights and humorists of the day—none of whom sought emancipation from earthly bonds off the Algonquin roof. (ed)

except that we all think we're invincible while we're riding high. I cringe to think of what will remain of my savings if the war ever ends and if my bank remains solvent. The many buildings I spent so many sleepless nights fussing into being will probably be bombed and demolished by the time this is all over. It's a wonder the cathedrals and the Eiffel Tower are still in one piece.

I know you've become quite familiar with New York, so I won't bore you with detailed observations, except to say I now understand why you went on about it at such length. But I do not share your passion for baseball, I'm afraid. It seems like a lot of screaming and shouting for too little in return on the field. I will admit there is a certain grace to it when the outerfielder [sic] maneuvers into position to catch the fly. But how strange—a game modelled after insect-chasing.

You were right when you said the buildings would make my pulse quicken. I have never seen such majestic structures. I have been in and out of more of them than I could count. I admire the instinct and know-how that inspires Americans to scale the highest mountains, as they say—but I must confess to having been vaguely nauseated by them also. First, it makes you dizzy just to look them up and down and take them in. Then, too, in their prodigious girth, they're rather monstrous and offensive—aren't they? Anomalous giants who exist to be gawked at as freaks of nature and are never allowed to belong to the real world. I do not think it is a healthy impulse that makes men build things so big and high. There's something inherently aggressive and destructive in doing so. I have always felt a mysteriously depleting sense of guilt (after soaring unusually high) upon finishing any project bigger than six stories. But that is me. I am probably the only person who has ever regurgitated upon seeing the Empire State Building.

Mr. Fitzgerald has been the host par excellence, except for a most uncomfortable half-hour or so in the middle of our first afternoon. He insisted on introducing me to his good friend Max Somebody[9], who is employed by the publishing company that has promoted Fitzgerald's literary works. I failed to understand why Fitzgerald was in such awe of this fellow, thinking he was so wonderful, when he hadn't been selling books lately. If this Max was such a genius, you'd think he'd be able to figure out a way to help Fitzgerald realize some income from his work, which Max's company supposedly promotes. But that is a different department, apparently. Fitzgerald dragged me over there to show me how it works. Indeed, he took me through most of the departments.

No one recognized him, so he kept introducing *me* as "F. Scott Fitzgerald, the famous writer." I smiled and prodded him to move on. It was quite crazy, really.

I wanted a cigarette, finally, and as I was fresh out, I was about to ask a janitor in one of the offices if he could spare one. To my profound surprise Mr. Fitzgerald went running up to him and clasped him by the arms. The man—who was unkempt and pushing a big flat broom across the floor—had been deep in thought, or distracted from a waking reverie. For a moment, the pale, slightly beak-nosed fellow looked as if he had no idea who Fitzgerald was. Then he smiled, and his bright eyes came to life, and instantaneously his slovenliness took on a genteel

9. Maxwell Perkins, the renowned Scribner's editor. (ed.)

quality, despite the frayed, loose salt-and-pepper suit and hair. The latter poked out of the corners of an old floppy ugly brown felt hat that was pulled down over his ears.

Then I realized it was Max, Mr. Fitzgerald's editor friend.

"Great Scott, this is such a surprise. You should have told me!"

"I would have, certainly, but I didn't know."

"Is something wrong?"

"On the contrary, Max."

"You've finished the new Hollywood book?"

Fitzgerald took a step back, with a shake of his head that seemed a touch impish, even juvenile in its overstatement. "No, no. This is a lot more than just fiction."

"Non-fiction?"

Fitzgerald came forward, close again. He put his hands on his mentor's shoulders. "My dear friend, do we truly need more stories?"

"There is nothing—"

"—so important as a book. I know. But in your heart, do you still really believe that?"

"I think so."

"Even when the world around us is crumbling?"

The older man nodded wistfully and gestured with his broom handle as he finished tidying his office. Fitzgerald let go of him and he leaned the broom against a large lectern piled high with manuscripts—it was perched like a sentry in the middle of the otherwise sparse office. "Especially now. Those of us who were destined to imagine a better world can share that dream with others interested in what *you* see."

"A small mutual admiration society."

"Discoveries of the inner country. Things of beauty that we live for. Do away with art and the artist, and you turn every man—no matter how simple—into a shell."

"I've outgrown literature, Max."

"You just need a new subject to write about."

"Maybe. . . maybe so. But literature has no intrinsic meaning in a time of global crisis."

I nodded, as did the gray-haired sage. Each of us noticed the other formally now, and Mr. Fitzgerald remembered that we needed to be introduced.

Max stunned me with a rock-hard handshake.

"It makes me feel guilty, telling stories at a time like this," Fitzgerald continued.

Max frowned. "We each do what we do best." His eyes flickered a touch mischievously. "Just add some social content."

"I want more, Max. Much more. If I survive this, I'll write about what Henry and I are trying to do . . . though that, of course, is not my motive."

"What are you trying to do?"

"We can't tell you—it's on a large scale."

"It's no big deal," I emphasized.

Mr. Fitzgerald did not take heed. He likened us to the nameless medieval artisans who slaved together lifting cathedrals heavenward over the vast European continent. Like them, we were bound to make our own nameless but essential mark in history. And we would become better men for it if we survived. Whatever our plight, Fitzgerald was clearly at the point in his life where it seemed "rich to cease upon the midnight with no pain" for a mission that could permanently dignify his existence. He struck a ramrod-like oratorical posture as he said

this. It was part of some favorite Keats poem[10] of his, Fitzgerald
said. His voice dropped an octave, to an over-sonorous artificial
tenor, as he intoned the long verses from the beginning, prattling on about a weary young man with heartburn who wants to
drink himself silly and fly away before his life becomes too painful to bear. Lovely language, although the sentiment was thick
enough to slice. The best thing to be said for it was that it didn't
make much sense (Fitzgerald wasn't giving anything away). By
the end, Fitzgerald and Max were teary-eyed. I guess I was, too,
though I couldn't tell you why.

"You're enlisting with the British," insisted Max.

"We may," Fitzgerald replied.

"Mr. Fitzgerald," I admonished, "what are you talking about?"
I turned to Max. "He's exaggerating as usual—though close to
the mark. We are going to write a film together on the courageous
RAF, which may mean we will get to go over—for research. But
that is all, I'm afraid. I think the British are recruiting slightly
younger men at this point. That's not to say we're not available!"

I broke the tension with a laugh, and Max and Fitzgerald
followed suit. If I had known that Mr. Fitzgerald was going to
babble like this with his old friend, I would not have agreed to
stop by. But it was too late for that now. The thing to do was to
bow out gracefully, making sure Fitzgerald's muzzle stayed in
place.

I looked at my watch and then nodded toward Mr. Fitzgerald. "Well, we've got that meeting at Paramount."

"What meeting?"

"You know—the meeting with Adolph!"

"Hitler?"

10. John Keats, "Ode to a Nightingale".

"Zukor!"

"Adolph Zukor . . . of course."

Max looked concerned. "Scott, you haven't been. . ."

This shook Mr. Fitzgerald to the quick. "How could you think I'd—"

"My apologies. Maybe it's me. I've been having a few extra myself lately."

"You'll see."

Quickly, Fitzgerald bear-hugged his friend, then broke the clinch just as suddenly, and held him at arm's length, grasping his jacket sleeves and gazing into his eyes with steadfast solemnity.

"What's wrong?" asked Fitzgerald's old friend.

"Nothing. Nothing whatsoever," Mr. Fitzgerald assured him.

Fitzgerald and I exchanged a quick glance—as if to say, "Little does he know." Morbid to say, but it's quite possible they will never see each other again—though that is the risk we have freely chosen.

(unsigned)

Hy,

Mr. Fitzgerald and I have just met with de Gaulle here and I must tell you we're both very upset. Who does this clown think he is anyway? Ghost of the Sun King?

He seems to think it's enough that he's stationed here in London, ready and willing to be carried home on the shoulders of his new recruits. Talk about delusions of grandeur. Hardly any of his countrymen would even know who he was if he hadn't managed to get on the radio—and yet it's so clear he views himself as the personification of France's every hope and aspiration. His vanity is as big as he is. And the man *is* big, I tell you, like one of New York's skyscrapers—too big. He tapers to his smallish head like a long balloon that's lost some air out of its tied-off end. And what a nose, too! I'm at a loss to describe the man. There's so much of him, you'd need a month of sittings like a portrait painter to convey the full effect. His aide-de-camp, de Courcel, received your directive, obviously, and the two of them met us in the baggage-claim area. Previously, I had detoured to the courtesy desk, where I placed an anonymous page over the public address system for our friend Alan from the State

"WHO DOES THIS CLOWN THINK HE IS ANYWAY?
THE GHOST OF THE SUN KING?"

Department—thus enabling us to slip away from him for a few minutes in the crowd.

I saw de Gaulle right away. He stood with a slew of the newly arrived, hunched over the luggage, looking as if he was searching for his bags. Even bent, he towered over the little Englishmen. He wore a heavy drab-green army-issue woolen overcoat, buttoned endlessly from ankles to neck, with a matching English-styled cap.

"Mon general?"

"Oui?"

His aide, a little man by comparison, interceded to inquire if we had been sent by Washington. I nodded, and introduced Mr. Fitzgerald and myself. The general had not heard of our organization.

The conversation continued in French. "We are young," I said.

"As is Free France," said the middle-aged giant, smiling.

"I must be brief, sir. As I knew we were connecting here for Paris, I had hoped to make your acquaintance; in addition, I seek your blessing and support in our endeavor."

"You have it, Monsieur Duval, as I hope I shall have yours in mine."

"What are you doing?"

"Doesn't that go without saying?"

"Excuse me. I thought you were referring to a specific mission such as ours."

"Which is?"

"Weren't you told?"

He and the smaller man traded inquiring expressions.

"No, sir."

"Mister Fitzgerald is going to meet the marshal and . . ." I made a gun with my hand and pulled the trigger.

"Are you insane?"

"Don't you approve? It will bring America into the war—immediately."

"Is anything wrong?" Fitzgerald inquired. As the General and I had been conversing in French, Mr. Fitzgerald had not been able to follow. In addition, a muffled drone of unseen planes was overhead, high above the clouds and fog. Arriving or departing? Enemy or foe? Almost everyone in our midst in the baggage claim area struck a dumbfounded, prayerful attitude, looking up and questioning fate.

"No, no," I said.

"Mon dieu," said the shocked aide-de-camp.

The general's brushy little moustache quivered with suppressed hostility, looking like a horsefly abuzz. "France will not be saved by the valiance of an *American*. It must be redeemed by the French!"

I was confused. I moved closer to de Gaulle, lowering my voice. "But if *I* kill him, Laval will simply take his place—and matters will be worse."

"Not you, idiot! The soul of the French nation must rise to this terrible occasion en masse. Otherwise, we will become a colony to whoever wins our battles for us."

"But—"

"And if you fail, eventually I will be forced to shoulder your blame." He leaned forward, pursing his small thick lips, flashing angry sparks from his hooded eyes.

"Henry," Fitzgerald said. "Really now, what's he yelling about?"

"You lunatics," de Gaulle said. "I would arrest you if we were on French soil."

"Oh, you would, would you?"

I was up to his navel—and our State Department friend had entered the baggage area. I grabbed Mr. Fitzgerald and we rushed away.

The General will appreciate us some day. But I'm surprised, I guess. I had thought he was a man of insight—an astute strategist. He just wants the limelight for himself—wouldn't you say? Lord knows, I'm not doing it for the notoriety. This is hardly glamorous work, being the doomed assistant to tomorrow's martyred triggerman.

(unsigned)

My friend,

I am on the train: destination Vichy. I'm with Mr. Fitzgerald, Alan, the State Department man, and a handful of fellows who look like spies (Nazi, American, French). We have been constantly on the move, mostly in the air, by military transport. My sinuses got all dried up from that cursed cold pressurized atmosphere, and now I have a terrible head cold.

As I gaze out at the swiftly changing view beyond this small window, I see that our countryside is still as lush and shameless as a young beauty in her first bloom, thank God. More than ever my heart pounds with hope as I anticipate the important events awaiting us in Vichy. This is quite different from how I felt this morning, upon our arrival in Paris. The Nazi flag is flying from the mast of the senate, the clocks are now on German time, and the world's oldest profession has taken on many new (and unseemly) recruits. The Germans are demonstrating their ability to bring out the best in us. Ironically, the Nazi soldiers in gray and green act quite friendly. They seem to have been instructed to make an extra effort to assure the vanquished that all is not lost, and that good things will result from this novel cultural exchange between our nations. We French are being encouraged to mingle. The children seem to like it. Nazi soldiers distribute chocolate bars, letting the youngsters get a close look at their guns and uniforms.

Still, the good cheer is no more than a fleeting impression, as neither party knows what to say to the other beyond trifling pleasantries. It is a forced peace, and though you can see the ugly transition slowly evolving—as evidenced by German soldiers and civilians alike eating with the remaining daily regulars at such establishments as Le Dome and La Coupole—a vaporous pall lingers in the air.

From the airport at Orly, we hired a taxi and took a short tour of the city to divert ourselves before our scheduled train departure at midday. Mr. Fitzgerald dragged us to an apartment where he and his wife and young daughter had lived on the rue de Tilsett about fifteen years ago. He got out of the car, and we joined him to stretch our legs once it became evident he was going to ponderously extend the moment. The State Department fellow and I stood there in deference to Mr. Fitzgerald, watching and waiting for him to be done with his solemn remembrance.

"We were happy here for a while," he said after the long silence. "I guess that's all you can ask."

"I envy you," I told him.

"But the soul is greedy. Henry. It always wants more."

"I know."

"You lose sight of the wondrous things you already have— at least I did. And I'm going to spend the rest of my life trying to make up for it—though I know I shall never be able to undo the knotted past. The rope unravels in my hands."

"Please—I don't mean to be cruel-hearted, but don't dwell on it. We can't afford to."

"I've lost my family—they're gone. I can never get their love back. I lost them."

"That's not a very good atti—"

"I'm going to die here. This country will be the death of me."

"It is not France's fault that you allowed yourself to become intoxicated with her. You did it to yourself. She did not—"

"All right! All right, already. . . But it's hard to believe it's the same place. It was homely before, but not like this."

The three-hundred-year-old edifice squatted there stubbornly, adorned with soot and grime. She was plain, and even ugly—but in an inviting way. Cleaning her up would have been tantamount to a public disrobement of a dignified old concierge. She'd live forever if the world would only treat her kindly. These old hotels—peasants with aristocratic pretensions—depend on us to love them. It's true that they look horrible now. Shutters bolted, shriveled vines in the window boxes, a pathetic blank countenance that mournfully announces her abandonment. She knows that most of Paris has fled.

The ineffable sadness was contagious. Once we were on our way again and the taxi passed under the Arc de Triomphe, I felt certain the old edifice would crumble on our heads. It is death imitating life here—a rosy corpse aglow. The cafes are understaffed and dirty, the sidewalks need sweeping. Tattered awnings flap idly in the weak breeze. At first, both Mr. Fitzgerald and I lusted feverishly for a familiar face, no matter how superficial the acquaintance. But ten minutes after leaving the taxi on Boulevard du Montparnasse, we decided we wanted nothing more than to lose ourselves in the crowd. Rodin's proud Balzac at the corner of Boulevard Raspail looked like a fool in this place. Any sane man would be ashamed to be seen here. I felt as if I were a priest visiting a brothel.

Mr. Fitzgerald looked for the Dingo Bar, where he had first met his friend Ernest Hemingway. He couldn't find it; superstitiously, this was upsetting to him. We spent twenty minutes walking around in circles. Then we stopped and had breakfast at Cafe du Dome. The coffee was watery and so were the eggs. Nothing was right, from the caning in my chair seat to the daily papers—so pitifully bland that I lost whatever was left of my appetite.

Afterward, we strolled over to a bookshop for the expatriates on rue de l'Odéon[11]. Fitzgerald looked at the store from across the street. He wanted to walk in and see if the proprietress (who is an old acquaintance of his) was there, but for some reason he couldn't make himself go over and enter the place and he wouldn't allow us to do so either. It depressed him to have nothing "in the works" (forthcoming, finished or in print?) to share with the lady. It had just been too long between books, and the only excuse, as he said, was that he had lost his promise—"and if you've lost it, you probably never had it to begin with."

I couldn't have cared less, as we were less than a minute away from where I had lived for years on rue Jacob. So many memories, Hyman, for both of us—when we were young, and

---

11. Sylvia Beach's Shakespeare and Company bookshop. (ed.)

the world was so new and fresh with inspiring novelty. Not the frivolous kind, either, but with such important and lasting experimentation in the arts. Who wants to think of it at a time like this? You become an ostrich if you dwell upon the past. Perhaps this is what happened to all of us. We became lax—complacent in our superiority as artists, innovators, bon vivants.

I could understand how Mr. Fitzgerald felt. Paris, in the early days, had been a ferment of celebration for him. Paris had been his golden fleece, representing everything he strived for: love, adulation, sensual delight, and a big fat bankroll.

We sought refuge in a stroll through the Luxembourg Gardens. It was eerily desolate: no lovers, apparent regulars, or doddering seniors.

The trees were nearly bare, and it was cold enough to make me wish I had mittens until the tinkle of children's laughter temporarily drew the curtain from my blighted mood. We saw a score of mothers and their brood congregated before a small portable stage by the playground.

The three of us went that way. It was a Punch and Judy show. Mr. Fitzgerald recalled the pleasurable interludes spent here on occasion with his daughter. Then, suddenly, everyone was howling with laughter—especially the grownups. The short burst of excitement expired as quickly as it began. According to Alan, Judy called Punch a Nazi in response to the latter's gleeful cruelty—at which the accused bellowed, "That's a compliment!" and plunged back into the domestic fray with enlivened zeal.

A morality play, eh? It was hard for any of us to know what to make of it. The show ended quickly after this. Mothers and children drifted away, mostly keeping to themselves. The muffled lilt of their chatter dropped like sand crystals in an hourglass until the park became a delicate, somewhat ominous vacuum once again. I have been in the Luxembourg Gardens thousands of times without incident, and I must say the mystery of my thoughts frightened me now. I simply couldn't put a finger on what it was.

Mr. Fitzgerald found the statue of Flaubert. He climbed up on the raised pedestal, hugged it to his bosom and put his cheek to the cold stone, wishing upon a star that doing so might confer a modicum of good fortune upon his present quest for le mot juste[12]. He extolled the virtues of the great novelist's painstakingly dedicated art when the sudden appearance of a couple of young Nazi enlisted men, wearing the standard drab gray uniform, shattered the nervous silence into a thousand jagged shards. They strutted along, jabbering boisterously in their mother tongue and bouncing on the balls of their feet every few steps as they alternated kicking a rock in the hard dirt—playing football with it and trying to outmaneuver each other and get to the object first.

One of them kicked it away as they reached the small, drained pond. Their noise was commanding. Fitzgerald stopped. We watched as they swaggered up to a man who was sitting on a bench by himself and reading a book.

The sight of these German soldiers—each in his dreary uniform, one with a rifle strapped over the shoulder, a pistol holstered—would have been intimidating enough. But you could sense they were looking for trouble by the curt way they sneakily lunged toward the man and tried to startle him.

12. Duval must be referring to Fitzgerald's novel in progress (his last), *The Last Tycoon*. (ed.)

"What are you reading?" said one of the Nazis, loudly, in passable French.

The man on the bench was small, wearing a plain suit with a colorful neck scarf. He may have been frightened but he didn't look up and he didn't answer.

The inquisitor bent at the knee to get a closer look at the book's cover. "Isn't the author a Jew?"

The man didn't answer.

The other soldier moved in beside his friend. "Somebody's talking to you," he yelled toward the disobedient fellow who sat there woodenly, not responding.

"You're one too, I bet," proclaimed the first man. He grabbed the book out of the man's hands and flung it into the mucky empty pond. Then he made a show of looking around, ignoring our presence. "There's no one here: we'll see for sure. Take down your trousers and let's have a look at your thing."

"You heard him," offered the second man.

Over my head, from the slight elevation at which he was standing like a sailor at the mast, Fitzgerald called out before either the State Department man or myself had a chance to stop him: "I'll show you mine if I can piss on you."

Surprised, as they hadn't focused on us, the Nazis whipped about in our direction. Scott was undoing the buttons on his fly.

"Stop!" I urged him. "You're going to get us killed."

The man on the bench took advantage of the distraction and sprang to his feet, running off. He had disappeared toward Boulevard Saint-Michel by the time the second German went after him.

The first Nazi wearing the weapons walked toward us.

"What do we do?" asked the State Department man.

"If we run, he may shoot us," I said between clenched teeth.

"Just stay where you are," I whispered loudly.

"Hello," the kraut was saying, in English now. "What were you saying?"

"I forget," Fitzgerald said, quietly.

"Get down from there."

"Can't you Germans take a joke? No, I guess not. That's the problem, isn't it?"

Then, in the same breath, using the stone bust of Gustave Flaubert as a fulcrum, Fitzgerald thrust himself feet-first from the pedestal, kicking out and striking the shocked Wehrmacht behemoth flush against the chest with both heels. They fell to the ground. The soldier's peaked cap was knocked off, and his stolid features were brightened by the flaxen mop that framed them. Fitzgerald bounded to his feet a split second before the Nazi, and stepped into him with a roundhouse right, the likes of which I have rarely seen. The kraut was pushing up daisies (at least for the moment) before his head hit the ground again. His friend knelt, momentarily distracted by the task of tending to his fallen comrade.

We removed ourselves from the premises with all the casual haste we could muster.

(unsigned)

Monte Carlo
October 21, 1940

My dearest friend,

You may race to the end of this long letter if you wish, but I won't rush the writing, as I feel I must relay the events in their exact sequence. Suffice it to say that I was only slightly wounded, Mr. Fitzgerald did not receive a scratch, and I am breathing the purest sigh of vast relief, as I can proudly tell you that none of our men was seriously hurt, thank God. Gilles and Gilbert sustained flesh wounds, but nothing so severe that they won't be standing at the gaming tables in the "Kitchen"[13] of Le Sporting, smiling tenaciously at the world as they bite down on their big cigars.

But I'm getting ahead of myself. Once we were ensconced on the Vichy-bound train, I got Mr. Fitzgerald alone and gave him hell. Of course, he had done the right thing, in a sense. I couldn't condemn him for coming to the aid of a defenseless human being. But he had risked our lives to protest an outburst of stupidity that cannot be dealt with on the individual level.

13. i.e., the main room of the casino, as opposed to the salons prives favored by those privileged few accustomed to wagering their idle fortunes. (ed.)

We didn't argue. We both knew the only way to go was to the top to stop Pétain and Hitler.

"That, and only that, will remove the Nazi swine from French streets."

"I know, Henry."

"But if you see anything else, you must hold yourself back."

"I don't know if I can do that."

"You must!" I insisted.

"I felt as if I would have been in complicity with them if I hadn't said something."

"I understand. But—"

"All I can tell you is that I will never abide such prejudice in myself or others again."

"Prejudice is at the root of human nature. We must fight it in whatever form it appears, be it racism, excessive nationalism, religious intolerance."

"I'm with you, Henry."

"I know, my friend."

"I hope we get them both."

"Pétain and Hitler."

"Hitler and Pétain." Fitzgerald intoned the words rhythmically, like an incantation.

"Yes, we hope. We hope."

The plan was for us to meet Laval and the Marshal at the Hotel du Parc in Vichy and then proceed by rail to Montoire, of all places. If I recalled correctly, the latter was a crumbling quaint medieval village frequented by eccentric antiquarians and its impoverished inhabitants—poor farmers who wore the heavy yoke of having been born and consigned to live there, unless uprooted by plague or war. A strange choice for an auspicious occasion, but my only concern was to make sure I made it.

Most of our operatives were there already, awaiting our arrival.

But first, Vichy. We were greeted at the station by a military escort who conveyed us to town in German automobiles. Vichy is no longer a health resort that exudes healthiness. Too many of the desperate elderly have frequented its hotels and mineral baths to little effect. A miasma of wheezing breaths expelled from decaying gums lingers in the air—along with stale perfume, lavender, sulfur, hazy steam, and heavy powder. It made me sneeze.

Our troubles began from the moment Laval corralled us as we were coming in with our bags—before we had even entered the building. Countless government types entered and exited, extending perfunctory felicitations, though we had no idea who they were.

"Henri! So good to see you!"

He was a small, stocky little man in his mid-fifties with heavily pomaded hair parted and plastered to the side of his head, then rising slightly in a small pompadour across his forehead. His unlined slightly oily face was broad and so was the bridge of his nose. A large Zapata-like moustache covered his thick upper lip, and a cigarette hung loosely from the base of his mouth, jerking about as he spoke, billowing tufts of smoke and thereby eliminating the possibility that he might attempt to smile. Nothing directly intimidating about him, seemingly innocuous.

"Pierre."

"Living it up in Hollywood, are you? You lucky scoundrel."

"What?"

"I hear you're living it up in Hollywood."

"I would rather be taking the cure here with you, Pierre."

"It isn't a party, I'm afraid."

"I've heard."

"And this is the world-famous novelist, Ernest Fitzgerald?"

"Scott," Mr. Fitzgerald and I said simultaneously.

"We so appreciate the patriotic support you so generously extend to l'État français," he said in thick, unctuous Franco-English.

We introduced the other American, who by now seemed to have caught a worse version of my cold—he was feverish.

Laval sent him off to be looked at by the marshal's personal physician—that charlatan butcher Menetrel, an idiot who still believes in therapeutic bleeding, leeches, and other primitive remedies. I hoped our friend Alan would survive the consultation. Then Mr. Fitzgerald was shown to his room as Laval whisked me off to an empty, ground-level office, which we entered from an exterior terrace. Ostentatiously, he shrugged more than once, adjusting the fit of his silky double-breasted suit, as if he were offering me the opportunity to admire his fine taste. However, it had the effect of making his appearance all the stubbier – not an impressive effect. His smug dark eyes glowed; he appeared to be holding back a hearty laugh.

"He cannot come to Montoire," said my superior, speaking loudly inside, as a beehive of human activity buzzed through the walls in the corridor just beyond this tiny room. He was talking about Pétain.

"You look as if you are joking—but why?"

"Poor Pétain. He speaks with his dear little heart but not his brain."

"He is our leader."

"Of course, but still he forgets," Laval said. "I am his daily reminder."

"What can it hurt if the American takes some notes and writes a flowery piece on our struggle?"

"Policy decisions will be made in regard to the British that neither Roosevelt nor Churchill should know about."

"Is that so?"

"The dear marshal is like a gentle grandfather. He is a great patriot, loyal to the cause, but not always an astute political strategist."

"Don't speak to me in platitudes, Pierre. You're trying to stop me from doing my job. Aside from infuriating the Americans, who are depending on Mr. Fitzgerald being there, this will make me a laughingstock."

"I'm sorry, Duval."

"We'll see what Philippe has to say about this!"

I left the rat standing there, and hurried out into the crowded main hall, rubbing shoulders with the antlike swarm of petty diplomats—domestic and foreign, clerks, government workers, civil servants—who scurried dizzily back and forth in the disordered maze of our current seat of government, trying to figure out where to go to perform their duties, lodge their queries, or register their official grievances. Laval called after me, but as soon as I was a few feet down the hall I ceased to hear him. I found my way up the main stairs and proceeded to the top floor, where I was promptly stopped by an armed guard, as I had chanced to venture in the right direction without a plan.

They lifted bayonets at me. "Halt!"

"Let him pass."

It was Laval, who had materialized from nowhere, such is his malign power, having managed to follow me upstairs in an instant.

I opened the tall doors and stepped into a small room. It was bare, except for a small settee with matching armchairs that faced a carved desk. Phillipe sat there in a high-backed chair, slim chest forward, narrow shoulders thrust back, his spine straight as a pole. His uniform sparkled with badges and medals, and his hair shone white as a cloud in the afternoon light coming through the close windows. He smiled with the innocence of a young boy.

"Philippe!" I said.

His brow bunched above his nose, and the laugh lines disappeared.

I realized his eyes were closed. Though his chin jutted forward with alert superiority, the eyes still didn't open. He was asleep—dreaming of what, I knew not.

"Marshal, how are you?"

"He's thinking," said Laval.

I repeated his name several more times, raising my voice until it was embarrassingly loud. I was reluctant to wake him with a shout—that would not have boded well for what I wanted from him. Alternately frowning, then presenting a pose of blank sanguinity, he maintained his ramrod-erect military posture.

"Perhaps he isn't well," I observed.

"Charles de Gaulle—de Gaulle!" Laval commanded in the rhythmic voice of the hypnotist or necromancer.

Instantly, France's chief of state awoke with a start. We were face to face. "Charles?"

"Henri Duval, sir. How are you?"

"Excuse me." His limpid blue eyes swam about the bare walls, seeking harbor in a vast mental sea.

"Marshal, did we startle you?"

"Pierre." His eyes widened. He turned to Laval. "Who is he?" he asked, nodding sidelong in my direction.

"Your assistant minister of foreign affairs, sir," I said. "I've just returned at your request. From Hollywood."

"HE WAS ASLEEP — DREAMING OF WHAT
I KNEW NOT."

"Oh, yes." He looked at me again. "What do you want?"

This was quite the reception. I couldn't believe it, but all I could do was to accept his demeanor as if it was reasonable. "I am sorry to interrupt you, Marshal, but I simply couldn't wait to say hello to you—so here I am, barging into your office."

"Aren't you that architect?"

"Yes," I smiled.

"I couldn't make any sense out of that sketch of yours."

"Really? I would be honored to try to show you what I meant if your time allows."

"Hardly. I am too busy signing *his* decrees."

He laughed shrilly at this private joke. I laughed with him, as it seemed appropriate. Laval stood there like a piece of wood until Pétain broke off in a cough.

"Well, let me show you to your room," Laval said then. "We'll all talk at lunch."

"But—" I started.

He put his arm about my shoulder, as if to steer me from the room.

"Where's the writer?" inquired the marshal.

"That's what I needed to talk to you about, Marshal. Pierre, here, has informed me that Mister Fitzgerald will not be accompanying you to your conference with Germany. Surely, there must be some mistake."

The old man looked to Laval.

"It's not advisable," said the snake. "We can't afford to make Germany nervous."

I spoke loudly to the old man, leaning forward to make sure he heard me. "But Fitzgerald's mere figurehead presence could do wonders for solidifying relations between us and America at this delicate time, sir. We don't want the United States to think we turned on England, do we?"

"Who cares about either of them?" Laval barked. "If for one second Germany thinks we have the Americans nosing around—in the open, mind you!—well, they'll make life tough."

"Don't be angry, Pierre," I said, "but let me express this one thought to you both: Would it be so bad if perhaps the Germans were to think that America was behind us?"

"An empty threat, Duval. You've been too long in Hollywood, and this is not the movies. Don't trouble yourself with matters of state, really."

"We'll see about that."

"Are you threatening me?"

I turned to Pétain, doing my best to ignore the snake altogether. "I'm tired from the long trip, I suppose. Mr. Fitzgerald and I will freshen up. We will see you at lunch?"

Again, the old man looked to his eyes and ears. "You have a large guest audience today, Marshal," Laval said. "There won't be time."

I stayed focused on the marshal. "Mr. Fitzgerald has some interesting ideas about that story you said you want to write."

"What story?" Laval demanded.

The old man brightened. "He does, does he?"

"Yes, sir."

"What's his name?"

"F. Scott Fitzgerald, Marshal."

"Oh, yes."

"You're too busy, Marshal," Laval nearly bellowed.

Pétain made a face as if he'd just tasted something disagreeable. "I'm hungry and I'm going to take my lunch. Also, Pierre,

I did promise the young man an audience, at the very least. He'll be disappointed, coming all this way, if he goes home empty-handed."

"Then where is he? We'll work him in with the others coming to pay their respects to you."

"He wants to talk to the marshal in depth," I said. "He's serving in the capacity of special correspondent for *Life* magazine."

"Too bad," Laval said, frowning.

"Don't be churlish, please," interjected Pétain, with reddened brow.

I saw that the snake's rattle-shaking was starting to get him into trouble, so I stood back and let him continue.

"After lunch you have your cabinet meeting, and then we must depart for the conference."

Pétain wasn't listening to him anymore. "I love the American songs from that era—the Roaring Twenties."

"Yes, of course, Marshal, but—"

"The Jazz Age, sir," I said. "Mr. Fitzgerald gave it its name."

"Wonderful, wonderful music," said Pétain. "Too bad it was all written by Jews."

"Excuse me?" I said.

"You know—Irving Berlin. Gershwin."

"What difference does that make?"

"Never mind. Just joking," Laval interjected. "Don't be so sensitive. People could get ideas about you."

"What does that mean?" I asked.

Laval: "Nothing, really. If you don't get it, it probably doesn't pertain to you."

"Hmm." I feigned confusion. "I'll take your word for it."

Ah, Music, the universal language! Prejudice never left their minds for a minute. Killing them both would be happy work. I was crestfallen that I wasn't going to be able to do it.

The guests had begun to arrive. You could hear the flock's excited trill out in the corridor, as they waited to see their French pope. I was whisked along with the marshal through a connecting door into a larger room. A half-dozen government clerks and factotums bustled in and out, carrying bags and boxes—the typical gift offerings for Vichy's visiting throng. There were cigarettes in gold metal tins, slim silver cigarette lighters, Baccarat crystal vases, bronze medals and miniature busts with the marshal's likeness, books, leaflets, calendars with state-commissioned photos or paintings of Pétain gracing their covers. One of the workers started yelling. His staff was preparing to dispense the wrong items. Today, the scheduled assemblage was a lumping together of local schoolkids, some scout troops on a field trip here from Marseilles, and a widows of veterans support organization.

"All's we want's the comic books an' a couple a calendars," the leader commanded. "Take the rest of this away."

He thought better of his nasty tone once he noticed that the marshal and Laval had arrived. He grabbed a magazine off a stack someone was carrying and rushed up to us. "Have you seen this, Marshal?" he asked in a disgustingly deferential tone. Laval grabbed the booklet from the fellow and began to leaf through it. I saw it was a child's coloring book. There was a broadly drawn cartoon of the marshal on every page. Pétain nudged Laval's shoulder, trying to get a look.

"Let me see, let me see," he demanded.

Satisfied that it had passed his inspection, Laval handed the comic over.

Pétain was impressed. "My, it's so nice," he enthused, indicating that I should take a closer peek.

"Handsome," I pronounced. I was at a loss what else to say.

Pétain's icy eyes thawed, brightening lustrously. He seemed to be waking to a pleasant thought: "We should give some paints and pencils with this, wouldn't you say? How's that for an idea, Pierre?"

The people coming to meet Pétain were pressing against the doors and outside walls. The fool in charge who gave the orders slipped the bolt aside himself, and a sea of eager, simple-minded humanity came pouring in. The widows I felt sorry for. There were just a few of them, and they played it up in black—hoping for a handout, I think, or some increase in "pension." Pétain had a guard on either side of him as he stood with his back to the open terrace. The draft was cutting, but it didn't seem to bother him. There must have been a hundred children. The scouts wore their little navy blue uniform knickers and tunics and were rosy-cheeked from the autumn chill. They hardly even looked at the marshal, but climbed over each other, clamoring for their presents, as the supervising adults screamed shrilly for order.

Pétain glimmered sporadically from within the nimbus of himself. He spoke once or twice, giving a short oration that inspired him to lift his chin higher, though the kids were carrying on so that his words were completely indecipherable. This didn't seem to phase him. But when he was standing once again in that nauseatingly exaggerated posture of vigilant repose with which he mimics an ambitious young soldier (unless you think he's in rigor mortis), a nearby widow's little boy of two or three came over and latched onto the hitching posts of the marshal's spindly legs with his tiny, sticky hands and clung to them for dear life. He was a cute, grimy urchin—stocky, with fat cheeks, wild reddish-brown hair, and a runny nose. He drooled a bit too. "Grandpa," he said.

The marshal looked down at the child. "I'm not your grand-father," he said firmly. He began to shake his leg. "Get him off me."

The child's widowed mother pulled at the little fellow, too. She was all a-blush. "Monsieur Marshal, I am so sorry—Daniel!"

By the time she got him free, the boy was screaming like a stuck pig, plaintively protesting separation from "Grandpa." Pétain administered a perfunctory pat once he was certain she had got hold of the little troublemaker. Then he nodded to a guard to move them off. He spat on his hands and rubbed them together. "A handkerchief, please," he instructed me.

I removed mine from my breast pocket and he grabbed it before I was able to hand it over.

"Did you see that?"

"Yes, Marshal."

"God, I detest children—don't tell anybody. The dirtier they are, the more they love to rub their sticky hands on you."

"True, I suppose. They don't know any better."

"Ha! Wanton creatures. Sometimes I think they proliferate with such maddening abundance just to mock us for thinking life can be a pleasure. I avoid them like the plague . . . when I can."

"Really, Marshal? We were all children once."

"Maybe *you* were."

An odd, odd man. I was wondering what he meant when a small boy bumped into me. He was a handsome runt, as boys go; from the looks of him, the kind I'd like to have some day. A cowlick, dirty knees, and a sweet devilish smile.

"Excuse me," I said for him.

"They told us we would get real swords," he said, speaking out of the side of his mouth, as if to imply that he had known better.

"Maybe next time," I told him.

He put his coloring book in my hand and ran out after a friend.

Once the adults had lingered to say thank you and touch the Marshal's sacred hand, they quickly disappeared. Pétain turned to me: "Ah, now that's a tonic for the ailing spirit," he said, winking. "And we still have time for lunch!"

He winked again. If nothing else, the Vichy propaganda mill performed its duty adequately. By hand-selecting just the right guests, they made the marshal feel his public was crazy about him. The kids even left him a few paintings of himself. Of course, being children, they didn't know any better—but neither did he. Once he had performed this intrusive nuisance of a duty, the old moron had such a look of complacency that you thought you had it all wrong for a moment. It was just a bad dream that we had been defeated. Pétain had really won the war—at Dunkirk, possibly. The Nazi war machine was child's play, just a little trifle that we'd straightened out with a swift kick in the pants—hadn't we?

I was given a little bronze medal embossed with the marshal's Roman emperor pose. Then I was shown to my room on the third floor. It was a shabby affair not unlike that little literary hotel we'd persevered with in New York—water stains on the ceiling and upper walls; ugly bucolic prints; drab, dark furniture (and not much of it); a beautiful parqueted floor polished to a slippery glossiness.

I was relieved to discover Mr. Fitzgerald there. The house

police had seen fit to separate us from Alan, the State Department man—who may have been deceased by now, for all I knew, given the "treatment" he'd received from that madman Menetrel. Fitzgerald himself was deathly pale; obviously, he was terribly fatigued from the endless travel of the past few days. I thought it best not to draw his attention to his ghastly appearance if he wasn't already aware of it. It would only make him worse, for the man—as we both know by now—is as vain as they come. He also lusts for conditions over which he can justify (however illogically) luxuriating in a good fret. A nice rest might help mend his lapsed condition.

I cautiously deliberated on how I might best apprise him that we were both going to have an ugly bounty of time on our hands now that Laval had pulled the rug out from under us.

"Henry?"

"Yes, Mr. Fitzgerald?"

"Why are you just standing there?"

I put a shushing finger to my lips while I did my best to explain the situation in a few words, as I was certain there were ears on either side of the walls.

"It's off," I said simply. "Laval killed it."

"Killed whom?"

"No one—our mission," I whispered. "We are not going to be allowed to accompany them to Montoire."

"Then we'll do it here."

"All of our people are either there already or on their way. We will be committing suicide if we act without having them in place to help us get out of the country safely."

"What are we going to do?"

"First of all, stop pacing."

"I can't."

He was moving across the floor like an insane duelist, doing about-faces from wall to wall. His shirt was rimmed with sweat under the arms and between his shoulder blades. You could barely separate his features from the soupy haze of Gauloise smoke as he sucked down lungful after lungful.

"We'll stall here until our security and surveillance return to Vichy," I said. "Then we'll strike."

"Look at my hands. They're flying away from me. I'm panicking, Henry."

"You've got to calm down. I can't stand any more of your antics. I've become a nervous wreck, too, you know."

"It's now or never."

"Shut up."

"I'm telling you—I'm losing my nerve."

"I can see that."

"Don't make fun of me. Both of us have put ourselves through as much strain as any soldier in battle."

"We're so brave."

He came at me with his fists clenched.

"Not that again."

"How dare you insult both our efforts."

"Stop sounding like you're speaking for posterity."

He started to angrily reply, but a bad coughing fit took his breath away, and he had to sit down on the edge of the bed. "I don't see that there's any other way to operate—that is, ideally," he wheezed finally. "But I'm willing to expend what's left of me . . . to shed my little glimmer like an aged firefly, if you will."

"An aged firefly," I scoffed. "Come on. What am I, your Boswell? Making sure you leave some immortal bon mots behind you—on the off-chance they don't march me out to the nearest firing squad?"

"Why not at least attempt to set an example for all of the other poor deluded wordsmiths, that one of their kind transcended his petty ambition and stepped forth from the quiet ineffectual herd to . . . to act like a good and decent ordinary man."

He had me pacing now, smoking like a chimney, quaking inside and out.

"So, this is it, then," Fitzgerald was saying. "No Pétain, no Hitler, right? We can't get our hands on either of them?"

"Right."

I went to the drapes, closed them halfway, and then opened them slowly—my signal to the remnants of our Vichy back-up team, Gilbert and Gilles, dedicated operatives on our side of the controversy.

"Get up, please."

"Why?"

"Just get up."

He stood. I lifted the mattress and found the emergency pistol planted there as it had been planned (a .32 caliber automatic). It was loaded. I handed it to Mr. Fitzgerald.

"We will approach his table behind the private screen in the main dining room, together. You will come up close to him, empty the gun and drop it. Then we will run out through the dining room and lobby, calling for help. A car will be waiting for us in front of the hotel. The driver will pull up and honk his horn as we exit from the building."

Fitzgerald nodded. "I'll keep my peace," he said finally.

"With the constant flow of people coming and going, we have a chance of getting lost in the crowd—but not a good one. I must stress that to you."

"Save it."

"I just thought you should know."

"You've reminded me of my mortality so many times already, I feel as if I've lived more than one lifetime."

"Good."

We shook hands, cheerfully, then showered and dressed. Though we both fully expected to die, each of us—quite independently of the other—wore the best suit he had brought along on this fateful journey. It was eerie. We walked downstairs, passed through the lobby, and entered the hotel dining room. Like the rest of this place, it was teeming with humanity—if you could call it that. Everyone's eyes were upon us, as most were excited by the presumptuousness of our destination, and hung on a thread, hoping that our arrival might provide them with a glimpse of their ancient god. We couldn't have been in a more conspicuous position, unfortunately.

Mr. Fitzgerald stopped to clutch his chest.

"What's wrong?"

"Heartburn."

His forehead dripped sweat. He walked with the stiff and awkward gait of one who is about to faint.

"You must sit down."

"No."

"We're calling it off."

He kept walking, listing occasionally like a drunken man.

"No." We approached the screen, walked around it, and found the snake coiled there, sipping his wine, and waiting for us—alone. "The marshal is a little peaked. He asked that you meet him up in his room. We'll eat there. Have some wine."

We declined the wine, so Laval accompanied us upstairs. The elevator was temporarily out of service, and the short climb was excruciatingly difficult for Mr. Fitzgerald. It surprised me, the way he clutched at his chest. Pressing exigencies had forced us to curtail our intensive exercise regimen recently; still, we had kept up with an occasional run, a few light sparring sessions, and some prescribed calisthenics. Fitzgerald had been in decent physical condition just a few days ago, and now he was huffing and puffing as if we'd never begun. We both smoked like chimneys, true—that might account for the wheezing. Stress, too, has been known to wreak havoc on the body, cracking open the fissures of old wounds and spreading them wide like flooded tributaries. Now, he looked worse than before. His pallid face had turned a painfully clammy spectral white; his cheeks were suffused with a purplish flush. I was afraid to say a word to him in Laval's presence. I became convinced that he was going to collapse on the stairs. Perhaps I was hoping he would, for our wheels were in motion—and, short of losing nerve and crying out our intended crime, this was all I could think of to stop us from surrendering our earthly souls to true treason. My heart beat like a wild beast, and I found myself surreptitiously clutching at my own chest—though obviously not to the extent that poor Fitzgerald was. Finally, he froze on the second-to-last landing.

Laval, dear friend that he is, noticed finally when we had left Mr. Fitzgerald half a flight behind. He turned, descending a step or two in phony supplication: "Are you all right? Sit down a moment."

"No. It's just these French cigarettes."

He dropped his cigarette, stubbing it into the floor. It was a dramatic moment, if I may say so. He seemed to regain his strength in the act of snuffing out the French butt. I lost all doubt as to whether he would go forward . . . and I was ready. This was the end, but it was triumph—it was dignity! I saw my

"...THE SHORT CLIMB WAS EXCRUCIATINGLY
DIFFICULT FOR MR. FITZGERALD."

life pass before me: my mother, my father, you, my brother, le Corbusier, some of my designs, my room in the Garden of Allah hotel, Mr. Fitzgerald (the first time we met in the men's washroom, when he tried to sock me), singing songs with Fitzgerald in his car, Marion emerging from the sea and shaking out her golden hair. So much.

Then, there were the same two uniformed guards on either side of the marshal's door. One of them opened it. I heard tinny strains of the most incongruous music coming from further inside the suite—"Sweet Georgia Brown" playing on the Victrola. Loud, scratchy, grating. The guards opened a set of doors, leading us into a dining salon featuring a large dark mahogany table decorated with oversized bouquets of multi-colored tulips, roses, sunflowers and birds of paradise. Covered globe-like silver food platters were placed about the table's center.

Then the old man stepped away from the table showing off a beautiful full length raccoon coat. Proudly, he waved a ratty pennant—that of Yale, rival to Fitzgerald's alma mater, Princeton. The name of the school was written in large block letters.

Pétain stepped forward and offered his hand. His empty blue eyes loomed large—wet and warm with fond memories of his own boom days, when he had reigned indisputably as a hero of war, the Victor of Verdun.

"King of my Jazz Age, I am honored to meet you!"

Fitzgerald reached into his coat, wincing as if he had been overtaken by a sudden pain. His hand jerked out, glinting with gun metal. He lunged forward, knocking into Pétain. Shots rang out—two at least. Pétain fell sideways. Laval jumped Mr. Fitzgerald, landing heavily on him. Fitzgerald was on his back on the carpet. I pulled Laval off, slugged him, and tossed him at the guards, who had not yet drawn their pistols.

I saw our only hope. I grabbed Fitzgerald by both arms, pulled him off the floor and pushed him forward toward the main room of the suite.

"Go!"

We rushed into the room. I latched the double doors behind us as the guards emptied their pistols into both panels. The balcony doors were open. We went out onto the terrace. It was a long way down, but we didn't hesitate—considering the alternative. A wide hedge encircled the periphery of the hotel garden; by the grace of a kind god, we landed on top of it, cushioning our fall. Gilles alerted Gilbert, who backed the car from the entrance as whistles blew and sirens sounded. More guards struggled against the clogged foot traffic at the entrance of the hotel.

I took a bullet in my right calf as we ran toward the moving car and Gilbert swung the right side passenger doors open so we could jump in. We caught up with the car and did just that. Gilbert was wounded on the lobe of one ear. We circled around the drive and picked up Gilles. They nicked his hand.

We got out of there. I'm pinching myself. Yes, it's true. We've been waiting for news, but still aren't certain. The old buzzard's been known to wear a bulletproof vest, but his coat was open, and I didn't see anything. Even so, I'm worried about it.

Should be leaving for Lisbon soon now. We'll be connecting to London, and then I'll send Mr. Fitzgerald back to New York. He'll be on his own from there. He will have been gone a total of five days. His girlfriend has been in and out of town on the gossip circuit; letters were written in advance to his wife and mailed in his absence; his personal secretary thinks he has been busy with story conferences on his new scenario project. He should have no trouble slipping back into his old routine without attracting untoward notice— unless we have failed, that is, in which case the State Department will probably do everything in their power to bury the very existence of our attempt.

For now, though, we left Vichy only a few hours ago. Mr. Fitzgerald is in the crowded gaming room just beyond the lounge area where I've been writing this letter. He's awash in his own triumph, utterly consumed with visions of his personal glory. He is attracting a crowd at the roulette wheel, making a spectacle of himself. I must go—

We're safe now, finally, I think—Fitzgerald's asleep next to me here in the cabin of this flying boat. We're waiting for takeoff. There's a full moon, unfortunately, but I've been told they're expecting some cloud cover relatively soon. Even if that doesn't happen, I'd rather be a sitting duck in the sky than wallowing in this little harbor. Can't see anything. We were ordered not to open the blackout curtains.

Ah, there we have it! I just gazed into my last glass of Moet—a 1911 (we began with a '28 Roederer). How I have missed our wines. Champagne, that gaudy vamp of an empress, a fleeting delight that makes the deepest, most lasting impression. It tickles you with the rarest, most serious pleasure—but you can't keep hold of it. A moment after one taste you must have another. And then she's gone, and the bottle is empty. If you chase after her it will kill you, so you sleep a long, dead sleep (your mind a dark and empty cave, devoid of any dream dust), and when you awaken you are so sad she is gone that you must seek her—or another—in the elusive effulgence of another frothy effervescent sea.

Fitzgerald won't be waking for awhile. Ordinarily, I wouldn't encourage him, of course, but I was desperate, since the sedatives I talked him into swallowing like candy had the opposite of their intended effect. I suppose he's become unaccustomed to them because, previously, I've watched him like a hawk, keeping him away from the incessant pill popping to which he'd nearly become addicted for both sleeping and waking. The sedative, in that case, should have been more effective, not less so. Or perhaps—and I shudder to think it—I got the Seconal and the Benzedrine confused. Whatever, the result is slumber—a relief, given his big mouth and grand manner. He had wanted to tell the world—or at least all of Monte Carlo—of our great (unconfirmed!) triumph. Barely could I impress upon him that regardless of our success or failure, there is still that little matter of our flight to sanctuary with the Allies—for whether Pétain survives or is dead, the war will continue. If anything, the conflict will be exacerbated by what we have done, at least for a short while—as we have hoped.

Mr. Fitzgerald became considerably less grandiose once his fortunes plummeted at the roulette table. You see, when I left you last, he was encircled by an adoring horde. He was "on a roll," as they say. Taking his life into his own hands for a just and worthy cause had rejuvenated his eroded egotism; after putting his life on the line back in Vichy, he lost his fear of risking something so vague and insignificant as money. He had begun with a few hundred francs, and being in that utterly unflinching, vainglorious condition, built it up into countless thousands at a blinding rate.

As I saw it, this silly roulette game had become Fitzgerald's metaphor for his life in general. I stood at the wheel of fortune with him, imploring him to stop, but he reveled in the ebb and flow of throwing good money after bad, winning big, then giving it all back. He loved every second of it, for his sixth sense was possessed with an indefatigable certitude that he would come out on top, no matter what he did.

At the high point, he had chips totaling well over one hundred thousand francs stacked on a special table they'd brought over to accommodate his prodigious effort. There was a maniacal placidity about him. He didn't seem to hear me as I begged him to come to his senses and desist. Under my breath, I prodded him, I don't know how many times: "You're drawing too much attention to us."

When he did speak, it wasn't in response to me, but to prophetically observe his most coveted hopes and dreams—hopes and dreams which had taken root (too deeply!) because of me. I have no idea how many Nazis were among us as he raved cryptically about his destiny to be recorded in the timeless annals of history as "a true hero, I would hope, Henry, not just a fine literary stylist, but somewhat along the lines of Charlemagne, whose love for the artful uses of language was exceeded by his tenacious love for France and all things civilized—it's what restored the Western empire after the decadence of Rome, of course."

"You've won a lot of money," I'd say. "Cash in your winnings and let's go."

"After all," he went on, "I can't deny I am now a man who has made his presence felt, a man who may have just fulfilled a very special, even divine purpose; after all, I may be the man—like Charlemagne again—who may have just saved France and the free world."

I coughed a great deal as he made these pronouncements; fortunately, the German floozie by his side was tanked to the gills—one of her straps was down on her beaded gown, which seemed to be enough to distract the other fellow in her vicinity (a dissolute, fey Spaniard in a frayed tuxedo and spats, smoking a cigar that was far too big for him). It was so irritating that she thought she could get away with pretending to be American by chewing gum and calling out, "Come on, baby!"

Fitzgerald hardly noticed she was there. He was too busy giving himself to charity, as his luck started to tilt the other way—quickly, to my vast relief. This was the only thing that could silence him, it seemed. He bet on the black and it came up red; he took the red, the wheel turned black. Sticking with one number didn't buck the odds; changing them was just as bad. He paled, then he turned morose. He was losing more than just a roulette game. He stopped tipping everybody; then he had nothing left. I was at his ear, besieging him with frequent updates of his abysmal position—but he shrugged me off. He shivered—he had sweated through his shirt—so he took off his coat, tore off his tie, and stood there in his sleeveless skivvy, perspiring under the harsh glare of the close spot hanging just above his head, in the midst of the slightly disheveled formally attired parasitic audience. I was beside myself once again with him, then, finally, he shook himself groggily as if he'd just come out from under a spell of sorts. He thanked the croupier and made his way through the small sea of admirers. I followed him outside.

The full moon lent an illusion of warmth as the vast inexplicable beauty of the Riviera shimmered before our eyes in the languorous play of soft light and stars upon water. Here it was, just a few kilometers away, that we had first crossed paths nearly twenty years ago—a couple of strangers with acquaintances in common who saw each other in passing and hadn't seen fit even to say hello. How time and chance make a shambles of our smug prescience. We have no idea, really, of what will become of our lives. It seems the more we plan, the less certain the outcome. And yet man is hellbent on conquering happenstance . . . mastering it, containing it, as if it were a wild thing—a tiger—and man the ringmaster whose charge is to subjugate the awful splendor of that which defies us with such dangerous capriciousness.

But it was cold. Fitzgerald shivered. I took off my jacket and handed it to him.

"Thank you, Henry."

"It looks warm, but it's cold."

"Like life, I suppose. 'O for a beaker full of the warm South!'"[14]

"What?"

"Let's have some champagne."

"What are we celebrating?"

"We're alive, aren't we?"

"No small miracle—true."

I called for service and had the wine brought to us on the terrace. They sent an old steward who probably slept with the

14. John Keats, "Ode to a Nightingale".

vintage in the casino cellar. He was so decorous, especially in comparison to the type of restaurant patronage I'd encountered in America, that his mannerisms with the bucket and towel were just too quaint for me. Perhaps, too, it is the latent American in me.

Surprising myself, I felt compelled to grab the Roederer from him, shaking it hard to get the biggest explosion. We caught most of the precious stuff in our crystal. There is nothing more liberating than the sonorous pop of a champagne cork under the proper circumstances. It's a belch from God, saying, "I had a good time—you're next."

I poured for us, then I lifted my glass. "My friend," I said. I paused, unsure. Then: "To the success of what we set out to do."

"Vive la France!"

"Yes, indeed . . . and Scott, please, we must be discreet."

"I'm no more of a rummy than you are, Henry."

"I wouldn't be so sure about that—but this is not the time to argue."

Bullishly, his chin dipped. A tight-lipped, pugnacious scowl flitted across his face—but not for long. "Right," he said.

Arms over each other's shoulders, we looked out at the cozy harbor lights along the docks, and the yachts nestled precariously in the larger, more impassive mystery of the evening firmament. Fitzgerald took his arm back and walked off, alone. In a moment, he turned back and looked toward me. "You knew what I was thinking," he said, frowning.

"What do you mean?"

"Always—even in there at the roulette table. I was so smug, wasn't I? So invulnerable to chance when I'm feeling my oats. Not unlike the monsters we so abhor—Pétain, Hitler, Mussolini."

"No."

"And it is we—the vain and narcissistic—who, according to the laws of nature, justly suffer the most ignominious defeat. If not now, then surely later at some point—God willing."

"You cannot count yourself among that scum, sir."

"At heart, through all of this, I never cared for France at all, really, or even the refugees of Hitler and his kind—you were right. Glory, my stupid dogged pursuit of elusive fame, not fortune primarily at all. I'm nothing better than a despot myself. You knew this, Duval. You pandered to my weakness, my terrible flaw. It didn't matter to you that I had disgustingly selfish motives. You may have despised me for this inwardly—in your soul of souls—but you knew you could take the weak, abject creature that I am, full of twisted, heroic delusions, and use me as a catalyst. You USED ME, HENRY!"

He was right. I knew it. And he knew that I knew. I said as much to you in these letters on numerous occasions. "True. I won't mislead you anymore, Scott, if I may be so familiar at this point. I have no reason to. But I don't dislike you—and I never did, really. I learned something from you. What it is, I can't say exactly, but perhaps I now see life—some of it, at least—through an artist's eyes. Over the brief span of our friendship, I absorbed your finer qualities—and they are many."

"How big of you."

"I value you as a friend, dammit, and I will miss you when we go our separate ways."

There was the longest pause. "Thanks. Henry," Fitzgerald said finally.

"The important thing, Scott, is that you have finally realized the truth about yourself. You're lucky—I wish I could say the same for myself. Because of this realization you have been freed from whatever illusions may have crippled you in your past. You've joined the world. You've embraced it!"

We clicked glasses, and then drank quickly and silently. Then Fitzgerald tossed his over the rail, and I joined him. The glasses shattered propitiously—perfect grace notes brushed over a snare drum. And then, Hyman, Fitzgerald knelt, facing the formidable darkness of the sky and sea as they seamlessly joined together, sheathing us in the mystery of birth, death, creation – all of the unknown worlds that we so crave to understand and love.

I joined him. He closed his eyes in prayer—and so did I.

"Let us pray," he said, "that we are closer to peace."

The engines have kicked on. The pilot says we're leaving. And so, we will cast our hopes ahead, our lives the bait, our actions the lure—for there is always another journey. But can we hook that angry leviathan without being swallowed whole? Your guess is as good as mine. It is beyond me to say. For now, I will do away with all lulls between battles; whenever I think of pausing, I will always bend my head.

Yes, let us pray, Hyman. Let us pray!

(unsigned)

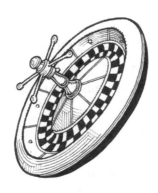

AFTERWORD

If Duval's memoirs are a true account of an undocumented assassination attempt on Marshal Philippe Pétain, then Mr. Duval's speculation that Pétain was known to wear bullet-proof armor is substantiated by the fact that Pétain, of course, lived. Whether Pétain was wearing the bulletproof vest at the time of the alleged attack is not known; whether any of the professed gunshots met their target is also impossible to say—though if Pétain had sustained a wound of any sort, it is quite unlikely that it would have escaped eventual entry into the public record.

After the liberation of France, Pétain was found guilty of intelligence with the enemy and sentenced to death—though, in view of his age, General Charles de Gaulle decided to follow the jury's recommendation that the sentence not be executed. Pétain was imprisoned in the Fort de la Pierre-Levée on the tiny L'île d'Yeu, below the Brittany peninsula, for the remainder of his very long life. (He would die on July 23, 1951, at the age of ninety-five.) He idled away his final days with long walks in the small prison courtyard, drinking Ovaltine, and studying the English language through correspondence courses. Perhaps, in his advanced senility, he was honing his skills in expectation that F. Scott Fitzgerald would assist him in the planning and writing of his projected opus.

But Fitzgerald could not have helped, even if he'd wanted to. He suffered a fatal heart attack just a few months after these alleged adventures with Mr. Duval, on December 21, 1940, in the Los Angeles apartment of Sheilah Graham, at the age of forty-four.

As for Henri Duval, we can make the vaguest of educated guesses. He is mentioned in the memoirs of several Resistance veterans ("Hyman," most probably, was the code name for an operative who has not been identified, as of this writing), though none consulted in the preparation of this book could say anything definitive regarding his present whereabouts. Apparently, he was involved in covert operations all over the Continent, from 1941 through 1945; as for his architectural work, his name appears in no architectural records in France or America after 1938. In *Paris Underground*, Jacques Remy, a Resistance leader, described Duval as a "melancholy man, with a slightly skewed sense of humor. He could make you smile under the most adverse conditions. You couldn't help but like the man. He bullied you into it, somewhat like a frisky lost puppy—but he was all business, too. You could count on him in a pinch when the chips were down; and he would never hesitate to lay his life on the line. He saved my life more than once with his quick thinking, and his hard-nosed attitude. I wish we had had more men like him. Strange, though, when an operation was over, he never hung around. He disappeared into thin air . . . until the next time. We called him 'the Ghostly Gent'—'ghostly' for his vanishing act, 'gent' because he had a certain dignified air about him. He was impeccably groomed always and comported himself with a kind of offhand nonchalance. He had guts and style; he was the epitome of a French Humphrey Bogart, I suppose you could say."

With the publication of this significant lost volume of correspondence, it is inevitable that we will be discovering more about this fascinating man—for the historian leaves no stone of truth unturned.

BERTRAND B. SLOAN
Princeton University
November 1983

ABOUT THE AUTHOR

Murray Sinclair is best known for his hard-boiled Ben Crandel series, a trio of Los Angeles-based mystery novels about a down-on-his luck writer set in the criminal underbelly of early 1980s Hollywood. The stories touch on the adult entertainment industry, political corruption, Neo-Nazis (circa 1980), and the moral majority led fearlessly by corrupt evangelists. The first of the three, *Tough Luck L.A.*, received the Special Award from the Mystery Writers of America for Best Paperback Original. In 1988, *Tough Luck L.A.* and its sequels, *Only in L.A.* and *Goodbye L.A.*, were among the few new books published by Black Lizard Books, the legendary crime fiction press whose selections are widely regarded as hard-boiled canon. In 2019, the series was reissued by The Mysterious Press.

To stay informed about the author, please go to:
facebook.com/MurrayMSinclair

A NOTE ON THE TYPE

The text of this book was set in Fairfield, a font designed
by Rudolph Ruzicka and released by Merganthaler Linotype
in 1939. It is based on the forms of Venetian Old Face
fonts as well as the designs and details of Art Deco
giving it a distinct appearance.

The display type is set in Love Potion, a font designed
by Hannes von Döhren of HVD Fonts. It is distinguished
by its hand-drawn and condensed style.

The interior and cover were designed and typeset in
Adobe InDesign CC by Jessica Shatan Heslin,
a book designer for many publishers since 1985.

All cover and interior illustrations were drawn by Rick Geary, an
illustrator for many publications including his own graphic
novels, with a Faber-Castell brush pen and Prismacolor
pencils on Strathmore paper.

This book was printed on 50 lb/74 GSM paper
at an IngramSpark facility.

*If signed, the first 195 copies of the hardcover edition
constitute a special edition signed by the author.*